Canvas Carvers
Following The Maven

I0666077

Written by
Maegan Alexandria

WILD REMARKS

Published by Wild Remarks Publishing
ISBN 978-1-5136-5072-2

Cover Design by Cihan Sesen
www.spinecomic.com

Contents

For My Husband,
and our long romantic walks to the fridge.

Prologue

As in a mist, two tall doors opened slowly, beckoning me to walk through them.

I didn't know where I was, or what I would encounter, but curiosity propelled me forward.

Suddenly, I realized something. I knew this place better than I thought. A quiet familiarity hung in the darkness and, as the path ahead of me began to glow, I recognized the scene instantly.

I was inside our chapel, with its cracked stone floors and empty pews. Only candles lit the way, as I walked forward with no real sense of purpose. It was as if I were being pushed toward something ... or someone.

A man with a black patch over his eye and a hat stood on the altar, slowly approaching me. It appeared as though he were gliding toward me in the same way that a ghostly apparition might.

It was Father Caius. The stern expression on his face prevented me from calling out to him. His bright blue eye was not kind, but severe. It was as though I had never met him before.

We almost floated slowly toward each other before he turned toward the right side of the church and faced the confessionals. The boxed rooms looked long and almost menacing in the dim light.

In my mind, I wanted to run - but my feet, similar to a wooden toy soldier, kept moving forward - and I was powerless to stop it.

Before I could make out what was happening, I was sitting in the confessional - not even capable of finding my hand in such blackness.

A slow feeling of suffocation came over me, as the curtain of the confessional whipped itself closed.

It was the middle of the night, and I was in a confessional with Father Caius - but why? Suddenly, there came a rough voice from the empty void.

"What is Andrew Godfrey's greatest fear?" the voice on the other side of the wall asked. It was a strange question at such a time.

"What is this, priest? Why am I here now? What have I done that I should find myself in our little chapel in the middle of the night?"

Only silence returned my question.

"Priest, please, what is the meaning of this?" I asked, my breath turning both rapid and shallow as the fear grew within me.

Again - I received no response.

Desperately, I tried to push aside the curtain - only to be met with a cloth that felt heavy and weighed down by boulders. It seemed that there was nothing I could do to leave the place!

"Please, Father Caius, please let me out!" I said, banging my fists against the wall. "I don't understand any of this!"

My voice was breaking, and I felt my throat tighten as the walls seemed to close in on me.

My greatest fear was not getting out of here alive, I thought.

After much effort to escape, I felt my knees cave toward the small kneeler in front of me. It was as though someone desperately wanted me to atone for what I had done - and had come to collect my penance. A lump formed deep in my throat, as my forehead hit the wooden rail of the kneeler with a loud thump. Hastily, I thought up one word ... one singular fear. It was the only thing I could think of at that moment.

"Larouche," I whispered. "Meir Larouche!" I blurted out.

All of a sudden, the confessional window between us slid open slowly. A large hand with a black ring on it slowly opened the window, and I felt my breath catch.

Through the grated panel, I could see a tall and dark figure on the other side. I began to realize ... it wasn't Father Caius at all. The man before me was Larouche himself, smiling cruelly back at me!

"You won't scare me any more!" I trembled - only it was too late. The panel closed slowly, and the walls caved in, capturing me inside. Like a madman, I began clawing and pushing my way out. Had I said the wrong thing? I panicked. Suddenly, I felt an intense heat take hold of me and crawl its way up my legs.

I looked down to find myself floating above an endless fiery pit, with embers snaking their way up my body.

This was hell, and there was no way out for me.

Chapter One
A Secret To Be Shared

There was a hotel, eleven stories high, in a deserted plain of dead land some miles away. It was far from the surrounding villages, but not *too* far that you couldn't become tempted by its radiance. Even in the distance it held a certain glow. *I* once lived there.

Though my time there was short-lived, the impact it left on me was one I would never forget.

To understand this, a person would have to know that this particular hotel possessed a certain dark magic within its rooms. Behind its walls, you could find a kind of magnetism so corrupt that *none* could be released from it.

If you looked closely, you would see smiling faces and frivolous dancing, masking the hidden lives of the patrons who resided there. These lives had been abandoned and lost, and most of the residents would *never* reclaim them.

If you looked even closer, you would find a man, a wicked puppeteer, who lived in the highest suite, looking down into the streets. He watched each zealot enter his hotel and grinned knowing they would never leave.

How could they? He offered them a wide array of delights that proved to be *irresistible*.

Only *once* did a patron choose to flee. Only once did a patron dare to remove himself from the painted pleasures that the hotel could bring.

A few weeks had passed since that brave boy left the hotel and only a few weeks away had left him with the most uncertain feeling.

***

I washed my face that morning with the coldest water. It was from a stream a few paces away from the chapel. A doe was nearby drinking from the same stream I was.

My life was peaceful now and if you looked closely, not too far from heaven on earth. We ate from the trees and breathed air untainted by the pungent scent of alcohol and cigarette smoke. Though the excitement was not nearly as abundant as it was back in the hotel, I was grateful for what we *did* have…because it was real. This life was *real*.

The church was our sanctuary; It had become home. Most importantly, it was our *hideout*.

Thomas, the lookout, was perched up above us on the roof. I hadn't known Thomas long, but he had been very close to Father Caius since his *own* father's passing.

A churchgoer, Thomas claimed the old priest saved him and his sanity from taking the high dive off the bridge at Stumptown Lake. He had discovered his father - dead in a large pit - beaten and shot in the head. Sometimes, I watched Thomas and imagined that he spent his days atop the roof plotting his revenge against his father's murderers.

From the smile on his face, however, I felt that his days were probably more meditative than anything else. We all sought freedom from our pasts, and I almost envied him for his spot on the roof.

Father Caius had crafted a makeshift hideaway for him to use, and I could tell Thomas was taking his job very seriously. He woke up every morning at five and left his post at midnight, keeping a close watch, should Larouche send any of his spies over to our refuge.

Twice we had encountered a few of Larouche's accomplices. They usually came to inspect the church, and would often stake out and hold poker tournaments in the pews. Their grand exits were often made by pouring whiskey on the floors on their way out.

We had all managed to remain undetected with the help of our dear priest. Beneath the church was a shelter, small but carefully concealed and known to hardly anyone. It was built for the clergy during times of war.

During high alerts, a small but piercing sound of a bell would ring. It was our lookout's way of informing us that trouble was near.

The sound sent each of us from our position in the church, running toward the safe dormitory down below. We would huddle together, covering our heavy breaths with our hands as we heard the lurkers footsteps up above.

We had managed to fool them into believing the church was empty - *abandoned*. It was why most of the food was kept down in the cellar. Any notion that someone was living there would have revealed our hideout.

Larouche knew we were out there, *somewhere*.

It was possible that he believed we used the church from time to time and that, eventually, we would feel safe, and take up residence in the old chapel again.

Why would he keep sending his men over if he had *not* felt that way?

With some luck, we managed to keep our sanctuary to our ourselves but we all knew it wouldn't be that way for long. Larouche was too powerful. If he wanted to, he could find us and bury us in the dirt beneath our feet. He was toying with us and, perhaps, luring us back to his beloved hotel.

We all knew that returning was not an option but Patch, my dearest friend, had his doubts. With no plan of action , he began to lose hope.

"I can't take it here any longer, Andrew. The food is *terrible*," Patch grumbled one evening, as we chopped wood together in a nearby forest.

"It won't be much longer, Patch. I promise," I consoled him, but deep down - *I wasn't sure.*

"What are we waiting for? I said I'd be by your side, Andrew, but not to waste away here!"

"It won't be a waste, Patch. *I give you my word,*" I promised him. He sighed.

"Eventually, we'll be caught. You think Larouche will ever give up looking? This is a game to him. It's best to leave the old priest here and set sail, old boy. Can't you just see us? You and I smashing about on the shimmering sea!" He said, shaking me by my shoulders. I laughed and shook my head.

"I already told you, I won't abandon this place. There is so much more to it, Patch." I said, with a concealed gulp.

"What *more* is there? There is *nothing* here for us. If this is about your loyalty to that old priest, then I don't understand you, Andrew!" He cried out, throwing his hands in the air.

The truth of the matter was simple. More than three weeks had passed since we arrived, and I *still* hadn't revealed to Patch what I knew about the hotel. I had yet to confide in him all that I knew about the mystical canvas, the altar boy who stole it from beneath his guardian's watch, and the lasting edifice that would always remain under his tyranny lest we fought to seize its magic back. I knew all this and chose to keep it hidden and close to my heart. Looking at Patch now, as he raked his hands through his hair in frustration, I felt terrible for it.

He was my friend, the very best one that I had, but I couldn't bring myself to include him in my secret. Selfishly, I wanted it to keep its value, and I worried that Patch would spread it across the plains like wildfire.

Father Caius had also expressed his concerns to me about sharing the secret with too many others, but it felt *wrong* not to include Patch.

Tonight. I thought. *I will tell Patch tonight.*

*** *

Patch came into our room that evening with his hair dripping wet. He wore a loose fitting shirt over even looser riding pants he found in a bureau in the attic.

"Nothing like a glacier bath of frost in the middle of winter," he chimed, sarcastically.

"'Nite," he said flippantly, blowing out the lamp on his bedside table.

The room was quiet. Not one sound could be detected, other than the wind coming in under the windowsill. At last, I spoke.

"Patch," I said, cutting through the quiet in the room. "I need to show you something."

Immediately, he sat up in his bed and kicked his feet out from under his blanket.

"*I knew it!*" He whispered, with great excitement.

In no time at all, we slipped on our jackets and boots and left the room. Down the spiraling steps, Patch and I crept through the church, careful not to stir the others from their sleep. It was not long after midnight.

The church felt hollow and lonesome as if not one soul had ever dwelled within its thick stone walls. With every slight sound came an echo that blended into our shallow breathing. You could even hear the flickering candles if you listened to them carefully. The building, dark and desolate, was in direct contrast to the radiant beauty found at the Hotel Larouche.

The Hotel Larouche.

As strange as it sounded, I missed the old place and even, at times, longed for it. It was a vice that left such a lasting mark; I wasn't sure I would ever be capable of removing it from my life. It was where most of my daydreams began, though I knew it could only ever bring misery. Once you drank from Larouche's fountain, it would flow through your body. You wouldn't realize how much you needed it to exist. I remember feeling desperate for it at times. Sometimes, I'd toy with the idea of running back but a black veil would cloud my dreams, and I'd recall my father's old suite and the demon inside it.

The darkness was mighty at the Hotel Larouche, and I wouldn't allow myself to get lost in it again.

Patch, I knew, missed it more than I. In my friend's demeanor, I saw a true loss when he spoke of it. He recalled all those that he left behind and those he would never see again. After a few days away from the place, we seldom spoke the old hotel's name ... but it never left our memories, and I wondered if it ever really would.

It hadn't taken much to conclude that Patch despised his newfound sanctuary. The church was so radically different from the hotel, so tranquil in comparison. I knew it was nothing like the lewd mayhem he so preferred.

In my nervousness, I wondered if my friends who had traveled with me would stick around much longer. Would Patch, restless in his surroundings, decide to leave? Would Valentina, so starved of freedom, eventually resolve to flee the chapel, too? In my heart, I knew there was nothing to keep them from leaving.

When the priest revealed to me the magic found in the cabinet down in the cellar, and the unknown history of a stolen canvas, it left me with an uplifting feeling of *rejuvenation!* Knowingly, I had sealed my fate by pledging my allegiance to Father Caius and in some way, I had sealed *theirs*, too.

When we left the hotel, I had offered them the possibility of freedom, yet there I was asking them to risk everything and join me. I knew my plan was not one that would be accepted readily and, in my fear, I refrained from involving them.

Perhaps, I thought, they would abandon this new life and their foolish friend, too. It was a thought that never left me.

Now, however, the time had come.

We took the short flight of spiraling stairs from our chamber to the church's sacristy, weaving in and out of hallways and tunnels as we went. Patch followed closely, as I heard him mumble behind me.

"You're lucky that I scarcely sleep anymore. I wonder if I'll ever go back to sleeping during the night again," he remarked.

"You can thank the Hotel Larouche for that!" I scoffed.

Since our departure, Patch and I seldom saw any sleep at night. During the day, however, Father Caius would discover us fast asleep and reprobate us for not making ourselves more useful. Patch found this *most* irritating.

In truth, the old man never made us work for our rooms at his small church. If he had, I'm sure Patch would have left upon our first day.

Wanting to lend a hand, however, I would occasionally remove the weeds from the garden or run a broom around the church floors. Valentina had made herself useful by repairing some of the old statues in the church. It seemed her passion for sculpting was not entirely gone despite her years at the hotel.

Noticeably, I sensed the old priest felt compassion for Patch and acknowledged that he was in a state of recovery from his years spent in the depths of a radical lifestyle. I, too, regarded this but knew far better. What Patch suffered from most was that of a *broken heart*.

All the while, Patch grieved for a love he could not have. His memory of Tansy stayed right near the surface when he shut his eyes at night. His dreams, I imagined, were filled with her visage as the love wrecked man often murmured her name in his sleep. Too proud to reveal that he still had feelings for Tansy, Patch never took to confiding in anyone. The act of baring his true feelings was emasculating and only served as a perfect indicator of someone's weakness. Henceforth, we would *never* broach the subject.

Similarly, it was the same way *I* lived. My feelings were my own, and only Matilda really knew how to pry them out of me.

I quickly removed any thought of her. I could scarcely bring myself to think about the girl back in Howell Village. Since I had gone from the hotel, something between us felt wrong and uneasy. I didn't feel happy when I reflected on what I had done.

I left her, I thought. *I abandoned her soul back at the Hotel Larouche.*

Though I saw her vanish from the mirror with my own eyes, something did not sit comfortably with me. What if she hadn't gone at all? What if, one day, she would come *back?*

In my struggle, I deeply regretted not taking the mirror with me. Though it may have no longer held any sort of light or trace of Matilda's soul, I wondered if there was something more to it. There *had* to be.

At last, we reached the sacristy in the far back of the church. Too dark to see, we each reached out and held onto whatever we could find. Finally, I touched a handle from a drawer and retrieved a box of matches.

"You didn't think to bring a *candle*?" Patch whispered.

Quickly, I looked for matches to light the few sconces that hung from the ceiling. Once the first sconce lit up the room, Patch and I both shouted! The box of matches fell to the floor and scattered around us.

Father Caius was seated at the table in the center of the room, drinking tea.

"Good God, man!" Patch exhaled, clutching his chest, and the priest crossed his arms.

"Mind your words, Patch," he scolded.

"Why are you just sitting there? In the dark? *Alone*?" Patch grimaced.

"I heard footsteps…moreover, I know a shortcut," the priest scoffed, with a smile. "I had a feeling Mr. Godfrey would bring you here *eventually*."

Patch didn't respond but merely slumped into a chair, out of breath. The priest laughed and served each of us a glass of wine. Instantly, Patch sat up in his chair, with amusement.

"*Wine*, Priest?" Patch asked, teasingly. "This wouldn't happen to be *holy* wine, now would it?"

The priest looked at me, rolling his eyes as if he expected nothing less from Patch, then he stood up straight and continued, "This wine is not *blessed*."

At that, Patch smiled and chugged down the wine. Father Caius and I watched him with all the pity one might have for a dying mule slurping up water in a hot desert. In seconds, it was finished. Then, Father Caius turned to me with a raised eyebrow.

"I can see why you may have prolonged telling him," the priest remarked dryly.

"I think he needs to know," I responded, and he smiled.

Crossing his arms in front of his chest, he looked back and forth between Patch and me, hesitantly.

"Know what?" Patch piped up, with piqued interest. Neither Father Caius nor myself spoke. We just stared at one another, wondering how to reveal our secret to someone like Patch.

Patch was different in that he was first and foremost an *opportunist*. The '*good of other's*' usually crept its way into Patch's mind after the fact. I knew this about my friend but I also realized that the old priest would need some convincing. He sat silently contemplating all of this before I spoke up again.

"He *needs* to know. I believe he may be of some help to us," I reasoned.

"He can barely help himself, Andrew," the priest said, running his eyes over Patch's disheveled appearance.

"*Still* here," Patch interjected.

Adamantly, I stood up and walked over to the cabinet. The beauty of its contents proved both alluring and overwhelming.

Daringly, I placed my hand on the wood of the cabinet and turned to the two men who observed me. The priest's eyes grew narrow with intrigue as he sat on the edge of his seat. Patch, in turn, froze with bewilderment - his eyes darting back and forth from me to the cabinet.

"Priest, I *trust* my friends. They came to this chapel without a word of judgment or ill will - just blind faith. I feel that those who have abandoned their old lives to join us should be included in all that we do," I began. "There should be no secrets among us. It's only right."

The priest's face softened, and he nodded.

"The most important thing to tell you, Patch, is that you are being welcomed into a secret that Father Caius has entrusted to me. Now, I wish to share it with you. This is unlike anything you have seen or will ever see. For the power within can change the world *forever.*"

I held out my hand to Father Caius, expectantly, and he pulled out a key from his jacket pocket. Through all this, Patch remained quiet and somewhat cynical, fiddling with one of the ends of his mustache nervously.

Carefully, I inserted the key into the cabinet's lock and stopped. Slowly, I began to twist the key until, at last, the door started to open. It moved gracefully as if it was opening itself and revealing its treasure.

Father Cauis and Patch both stood up with overwhelming anticipation.

When the doors opened, a gust of wind flew out, nearly knocking us over. Two large clouds and a bright blue sky filled the room so magnificently that it was as if we were soaring among the clouds!

Flowers bloomed and the sun shone so brightly that we all had to shield our eyes from its powerful rays. Warmth instantly spread over everyone in the room. The plain fact that we were *indoors* seemed unfathomable beneath such clouds. This was a perfect day outdoors, somehow breathing and finding life within in a sparse room that was only accustomed to the darkness. As I gazed upon it, I felt my mouth spread into a genuine smile.

Remembering my friend, I turned to find Patch overwhelmed and speechless, lost in the canvas's beauty. His stunned expression led me to believe that he was overcome by what he witnessed.

"*What is this magic*?" Patch asked, reaching out to touch the clouds. The priest, who was preoccupied with gazing up at the live tableau, mumbled a response.

"*This* is how the Hotel Larouche came to be. This is how it still stands as beautiful as it did nearly forty years ago."

"It's *spectacular*!" Patch nearly hummed, running his hands through the flowers.

After a moment of feeling the warmth on our faces, the priest pushed the clouds and the flowers back into their cabinet. Together, we lassoed in the sun using a few loose chords from some of the hanging garments.

After the cabinet was closed we stood there, each too stunned to speak. Finally, I locked the doors in silence, wishing I could bask in the tableau's beauty forever.

Patch sank into his seat, unable to comprehend anything he had just seen. The priest sighed, heavily.

"That is the fourth time I have seen it in my life, and each time feels like the first," the priest beamed.

"But, how can this *be*? How, priest, do you have a piece of the sky in your *closet*? Real sky! As real as you and I!" he exclaimed, raking his hair through his hands. He continued, "Tell me before I go mad!"

The priest and I looked at each other, each deciding where to begin. At last, the priest sank back into his chair.

"The tale of the magic is a long one, best left for another night. What you must know is this. We are in pursuit of a canvas - a unique canvas that creates this kind of magic. We believe Larouche has kept it hidden somewhere in the hotel."

"A *canvas*? You mean, what *painters* use?" Patch asked, in disbelief. Quickly, I nodded.

"When you paint on it, your renderings come to *life*. Anything you can dream of is materialized."

"So you see why such an object has the potential to ruin humankind. The Hotel Larouche is proof alone," the priest spoke up, and Patch immediately came to his feet. He paced about the room, breathing heavily.

"How did Larouche come to have it?" he asked. Father Caius responded as he sat up in his chair.

"The roll of hemp used to create this canvas was stolen from me years ago. Meir Larouche was an altar boy in this church. One night, he left with a few other stolen valuables. My assumption is that he has it and has discovered how to manipulate it ... however, he does not work alone."

Patch stopped his pacing and lifted an eyebrow. "*Harvey Nicholas.*" he whispered, with realization.

"Perhaps," I agreed. "I hope you understand now. *This is* why I couldn't leave, Patch. You must believe that I wanted to tell you, but I couldn't. I didn't know how," I admitted.

Patch looked at me, slightly wounded. He crossed his arms in defense.

"With your help," I continued. "I'd like to go back to Larouche."

"*Go back?*" Patch asked, as if I had just uttered the most incredulous idea. "They'll tear you apart, Andrew! You can't go back!" Patch argued.

"Honestly, I can't imagine a better person to lead us to the canvas," Father Caius interrupted.

I looked at Patch, who stared at the old priest in disbelief. After a moment, he rested his shoulders reluctantly. I could practically hear his thoughts zigzagging back and forth in his mind, as he tried to comprehend everything.

"You two are fools if you think you will come out of this alive. Larouche will never have it. It 's a death wish!"

"Perhaps," I responded. "I was hoping I might have you there with me, by my side. As you say, no one knows the hotel better than you."

Patch looked back and forth from Father Caius to me, as if he wanted to say something. All that he had seen surely given him a new perspective on our current situation, but I couldn't make out what he felt. Deep down, however, I knew it was in his nature to resist any ties he felt to a singular person or situation. If it was not his Tansy, he could not find it in himself to commit.

Father Caius didn't waste a moment. He pulled out a small notebook and quickly procured a writing utensil.

"Is there a plan?" He asked, hesitantly. The priest and I looked at each other with a knowing look.

"Not one that ends in anything other than bloodshed," the priest sighed. "I can't imagine a way out once we've gone through the doors of the hotel. It would be difficult, indeed."

For a moment, I could see Patch thinking about what the old man had said. A gleam of possibility could be found in his eyes.

"Count me in!" Patch proclaimed, rather bombastically. "I've always enjoyed creating a riot!"

"We're outnumbered, Patch. It would be a suicide mission, and if we die …the secret of the canvas dies with us. There must be another way in … one that *doesn't* require weapons."

With that, Patch rolled his eyes and sank into a chair with defeat. Noticing this, I spoke up.

"But I do hope to have you join us, Patch. I understand that you are free to live as you choose but to fight for something greater than yourself … well, a person doesn't get that chance too often."

"If we were *fighting*, I would be inclined to agree with you," he retorted.

Father Caius interjected, "In our own way, we will be."

The old priest continued scribbling away, and Patch and I both strained to read what he was writing.

"It is my last will and testament," the priest said, nonchalantly.

"But why?" Patch and I both nearly gasped.

"Well, despite whether or not you two would like to acknowledge it I am advancing in my years. Moreover,

I cannot be confident about what lies ahead for me. I need to secure my possessions with someone."

"The *canvas?*" Patch asked, and the priest shook his head.

"The canvas never belonged to me. It belongs to *humanity*."

"But certainly it needs an overseer. Someone to make sure that what is painted on it benefits humanity," I argued, but the old priest merely smiled.

"Not an overseer, Andrew. An *artist.*"

Over the past few weeks, Father Caius had come to know my hidden passion for drawing. Somehow, I felt as though he had always known it. Perhaps, it was the reason he showed me the canvas in the first place.

Often, the old priest would ask to see my drawings or peer over my shoulder as I drew in my sketchbook. It was as though he were examining my abilities, under a critical eye. Now, I understood why.

"*Me?*" I asked. Patch was just as lost as I was.

"*You*, Andrew. We've known it all along. Only someone as good-natured as you, with your abilities, could ever lead such a rebellion. A quest like this one can only be accomplished by someone with an artist's hands," he said, reaching for my own pair, and holding them up for all of us to examine. Patch squinted as he looked at them, clearly finding them to be nothing more than an ordinary pair of hands. Then, he looked at his own.

"Am I missing something?" He asked, but Father Caius brushed his question off with an another inquiry.

"Will you lead us?" He asked me, and we all fell silent.

To lead others required something I didn't have — *belief in oneself.*

In truth, it didn't feel right to take on such a task. Who was I? I didn't lead my own life, so how was I expected to shepherd the others? Overwhelming fear gripped me.

There was no answer, no word of acknowledgment from me whatsoever as I left the sacristy that night. I didn't say no and yet, agreeing felt *foolish.*

In my youth, I was nothing but an outcast. Now, I was expected to influence the world with my brush, while molding new possibilities.

As I lay in bed later that night, I looked at my hands, only lit by the moonlight. In vain, I noted nothing particularly spectacular about them. They seemed like plain ol' hands to me!

The priest noted something special in them, however, and I wondered how he could identify my hands as being artistic and unique. As I shifted them back and forth in the light, I tried to see what *he* saw.

Nothing. There was nothing found in my hands, nothing found in my heart, and nothing found in my past that would convince me to be their leader.

CHAPTER TWO
VISITORS

"The world has turned against you, Andrew Godfrey."

I cracked open my right eye to find Patch, in his usual tattered clothing, staring at me from behind the lens of a long telescope. He'd discovered the old thing tucked away behind some old furniture in our small room. He swiveled the telescope back and forth, peering through it as if it was the most extraordinary object he'd ever beheld. I suppose it *was* these days.

"A boy, hated in his village, and thwarted from the Hotel Larouche. You're not welcome anywhere, so what will you do?" Patch jeered. He continued,

"You can't run, Andrew Godfrey - though I've suspected you weren't planning to anyway. But now you face an obstacle that has you terrified. You sit awake during the morning's dawn and ponder over *everything*," Patch smiled, as he saw my embarrassment. "Here I am, wondering the same thing. *What will he do?*"

Before I could answer, I stopped. Patch stopped, too. We both listened, straining our ears for a familiar, unwelcome sound — a bell.

Intruders!

Not too far in the distance, a signal could be heard. We looked at each other for a moment before we started hiding our belongings.

"Quickly, Andrew!" Patch warned. He opened the door, and we rushed out of our room.

Together, we bounded down the stairs taking them two by two. Rustling sounds and frantic whispers came from down below. I could see Valentina and the guardsmen, Birch and Gideon, huddled around Father Caius.

"What is it?" I whispered, rushing at them.

"The key to the cellar," Valentina said, quite shaken. "Patch was down here last."

"The key … I left it on the nightstand!" he panted, his voice quivering slightly. Patch instantly turned around to retrieve the key, when the old priest stopped him.

"It's too late!" He called out to him. Then, he looked around at us all.

Valentina stood beside him, her hands fiddling together out of fear. She looked at me, and I smiled at her for reassurance, but even *I* knew that we were all in considerable danger. What could we do now?

This scare was no different the first one that occurred during our second day at the chapel. Nearly twenty parishioners all knelt down in prayer led by Father Caius, while we suppered in the kitchen.

We weren't there long before we noticed something peculiar in the air that surrounded us.

"*Smoke*," Patch said, looking at me, just as screams and shouts sounded from the chapel. We all ran toward the source of the fire, while some of the parishioners gathered buckets of water from the well. Banding together, we grabbed all the blankets we could find to put out the fire It was fortunate that no one was hurt that night, and that we managed to save the chapel from burning to the ground.

Father Caius, however, decided that mass would resume when all was safe. He feared that the fire was only the first of many attacks that the parish would undergo and wasn't prepared to risk the lives of the devout community. It was *then* that Thomas volunteered to be the parish's lookout.

Somehow, banding together had proved to work at such a time, but I couldn't be certain that it would work again. Who knew what weapons they would unleash upon us, or how they would plan to terrorize our group next. The risks were great, and the cellar proved to be the best hideaway.

There we stood, however, minutes from facing the intruders without a key. It would be a *death march* if we didn't act fast.

"Hurry, there's no time to waste," I heard myself command. "Grab something to use. We *must* try and defend ourselves!"

Altogether, we fled in different directions, frantically. Each of us grabbed brass candelabras and iron pans to use in our weak defense against Larouche's men.

For the first time in days, I saw Patch move with purpose and excitement. He saw this as a great opportunity and a sporting chance to use his god given abilities in combat.

What sort of army were we, with our household objects, against their vast array of *sizable weapons*? I shuddered at the thought of our slain bodies spread around the floors of the church. No one would know the purpose we had each served or the mission we had set out to accomplish. We would die mercilessly, and Larouche would win again.

As I rushed to the front of the church, I felt the adrenaline buzz within me. I couldn't shy away in fear, even in the face of death. As Patch stood beside be, armed with a large shovel, I knew he felt the same.

The pounding of a fist against the door resounded in the near empty church.

With all of us scattered about, my shattered nerves intensified. The word "retreat" was at the tip of my tongue.

It was too late. The doors burst open with a strong gust of wind. Blinding rays of sunlight poured in, and a horrid smell of rotting flesh instantly followed. The intruder barged through the church, and his large boots scuffed the wooden planks violently. What sizable army followed him?

His quick and determined steps only led me to believe one thing. The man has come for us all and *nothing* would stop him.

CHAPTER THREE
THE UNVEILING

Behind the beams of sunlight, the man came forth. As he drew closer, I noticed that he was carrying a bundle in his arms. I saw, with great relief, that the man was someone strikingly familiar to me - someone that I'd left back at the hotel.

My father!

"Alben!" Father Caius nearly sang as he met my father in the middle of the church. The priest rushed toward him.

"Please, she needs help," he said, his forehead dripping with sweat.

"Of course," Father Caius said motioning toward the stairs.

Stunned, I stood there in disbelief. After nearly three decades, my father had finally left the hotel with my sister, but I didn't know why.

I saw that her eyes were closed, as sleep overtook her. My father, tired but alert, looked stunned, as he noticed my presence in the old church.

"Andrew? Is that you, boy?" he asked with a half smile. I nodded, then I saw him recognize Patch, who stood beside me.

"I thought you two were in Howell Village! How have you come to find this old church?" He asked further. Before my father's questions were answered, however, Father Caius intervened.

"Come, Alben. Let's take the girl to Valentina's room. We shall prepare a bed for her."

My father, looking down at the girl in his arms, suddenly realized why he had come.

"Anais has become weak from the wounds, Father. No one would treat her."

"I can't say I'm surprised," the old priest sighed.

"What can we do?" he pleaded.

"Send for a doctor, immediately," he replied. Patch's eyes widened.

"You don't think Larouche has infiltrated the post? We'll be discovered in no time," he argued, but the old man merely shook his head in response.

"This girl will not live long unless we do something now. We must bring help unless you can think of a better solution," the priest said, almost challengingly.

I didn't know how much Father Caius knew about Patch's history, but the fact that a talented doctor of our own was in our presence didn't escape me. I looked at Patch who rubbed his neck as he turned away, with embarrassment.

Patch had previously been a practicing physician years before I encountered him back at the hotel, but he had since appeared to have given it up. The room grew silent as we all waited for him to respond, but Patch remained quiet.

The priest led my father and my sister to the back of the church and up the stairs. I saw familiar worry written upon my father's face. It was the same worry he had back in his suite that day - the night of Anais's recovery. Together, Valentina and Father Caius's two blind guardsmen, Birch and Gideon, followed them.

I realized that Patch had chosen to stay behind. Turning to him, I saw him look at the ground, then the floor. He looked everywhere but at me.

"Are you not coming, then?" I asked, slightly baffled with Patch's hesitation. He shook his head.

"No, I don't think I will."

"The Hell you will!" I heard myself shout. "Anais - *my sister* - needs you. She'll die if she doesn't get help and yet, you'd risk our exposure for your own self preservation!" I nearly spat.

Patch looked at me as though I had just jabbed him in the stomach. He didn't speak, but I did.

"You've been moping about here for days. If you don't wish to help then *go*.   No one will hold you back, lest of all me." With that, I left him standing there alone with his guilt.

Quickly, I bounded up the stairs and made a sharp left toward Valentina's room. My sister was already lying in bed and our father sat beside her, calmly wiping the sweat from her forehead. Now awake, she moaned slightly and held out her arms to my father. Although she was in much better spirits than our last encounter, she still grimaced in pain. It was at this moment that I first noticed how *similar* we were. Our thick wild hair and pallid skin alone instantly paired us as siblings.

At first, I couldn't be sure if she recognized me, but a quick lingering glance my way gave me all the answers I needed. She may not have known where she knew me from, but I was a familiar face nonetheless.

Valentina entered the room with a large basin and some rags, followed by Father Caius.

The old priest looked at my sister with all the sympathy in the world - careful not to touch the scars that covered her rail-thin limbs.

"You poor girl," the priest sighed. "We pulled you out of the darkest pit in Hell, and now *this*."

"Andrew, send for a doctor," my father commanded.

"Wise decision, Alben," Father Caius agreed.

Before I could go, Birch and Gideon walked into the room, with blanched faces.

"You can't go, Andrew," Gideon warned. "We spoke with one of the parishioners. They said Larouche has the town infiltrated with *spies.*"

"Larouche knows I've left by now. He *must.*" My father spoke to the room. "There's a war on our hands. If he knows we're together, he'll come looking for us himself and put an end to any revolution he thinks may be occurring. You don't leave his hotel, and live to tell others about it."

My father's eyes looked lost in thought, as though he had feared his departure from the hotel for many years. I wondered if he knew anything about the canvas Larouche was using, and the magic we were fighting to preserve.

My sister started crying and wincing, as she held her side. Blood leaked out onto her gown, which was previously stained from past wounds. Valentina and I rushed to the bed, followed by Birch and Gideon - each wanting to assist, but none of us knowing where to begin.

"For the love of mercy, this isn't the Black Death you're dealing with! It's just a few wounds that need bandaging; that's all!"

Patch stood at the door with his arms crossed. He threw the entire group an irritated look, before shoving his sleeves up to his elbows with an arrogant scoff. Immediately, he darted over to my sister, who was still whimpering from the wound. In silence, he looked down at her.

Patch, grabbing the bandage from my father, knelt down beside her. "Someone get me an egg, turpentine, and some rum!"

"Rum?" Father Caius asked.

"That's for me," Patch responded, and Father Caius threw me a knowing look.

Valentina, Birch, and Father Caius left at once, their footsteps echoing in the hallway as they went. Only my father, Gideon, and I remained as spectators. We all stood still as we watched Patch tear the fabric of my sister's gown, directly over a large wound. It seemed as if there was not one spot on her body free from a gash or scar. The primitive life she lived was ever present on her form and only served to remind the world of where she came from.

Wearily, my father looked around the room at the people that surrounded him. Having escaped the Hotel Larouche, he couldn't believe that he had made it to the chapel.

Grabbing the carafe of water sitting on the side table, I poured my father a drink and he took it gladly.

"Everything happened so fast," he relayed, and I nodded. "This morning I woke up, looked at my dying child and knew that we'd had enough."

"You did the right thing, Father," I responded. "She'll be in good hands here."

We had rescued Anais from the darkest of places, and a hole in her soul permeated with demonic creatures and their masters. Now, all that was left were battle scars from the brutality of the Hotel Larouche.

Slowly, I walked around the bed and stood by Patch, whose focus never drifted from my sister's wounds.

"Not a word, Andrew," he warned, and I smirked.

My father leaned against one of the walls, as his constant worried expression seemed to melt right off his face. Then, he looked at me, and his body stiffened. Discretely, he motioned toward the hallway outside.

He left the room, and I followed him, making way for Valentina and Birch as they slipped past us with the ordered medical supplies.

When my father closed the door, he turned to me, prepared to speak. Father Caius, who was making his way down the hallway, held up his hand when he saw us. It was his way of preventing my father from talking.

"He knows, Alben," the priest said, and my father looked at me with wide eyes that relayed complete surprise. "He's here to help. They all are."

My father looked at the old priest for a moment, then his eyes narrowed in on me.

"This is no simple task, Andrew. It would be best if you went back to Howell, where you belong," he warned. I felt my shoulders slump as I took a step back.

"You don't think I can do this," I responded to his warnings, feeling an instant *hurt* that I hadn't expected.

Father Caius saw this and interjected in the conversation by suggesting that my father take a look at my drawings.

"You will find that they are outstanding," the old man praised. "How can we expect to go any further without an artist fighting by our side? We *need* him, Alben."

My father looked at the both of us standing there in the darkened hallway. His skepticism was not lost on me. Though I had not known my father long, I knew that he was a man who played his cards close to his chest. He suffered and lost nearly all those whom he loved with all his heart. To him, nothing fraught with any danger was worth doing.

Nervously, I could see him formulating a decision in his mind. A resilient man, my father took cautious steps. I only prayed they were in *my* favor.

"*Show me*," he ordered, his voice just above a whisper.

Together, we walked to the end of the hallway, and I pushed open the door. The room was well lit by the few bursts of light peering through our opened windows.

Oddly nervous, I held open the door for my father and the old priest. It was as though I were sharing my intimate dreams and imaginings with them. It was as though a door had been unlocked into the cavities of my mind, as my amateur renderings were suddenly on display.

My father walked in, tentatively at first. It only took him a mere moment, however, for him to realize that *I* had created all the illustrations and oil paintings scattered about the room haphazardly. He studied and scrutinized each one, marveling at them as if they relayed the most important of anecdotes.

If only he had known that each portrait and landscape was *not* so carefully crafted. There was no significant history or momentous tale behind each painting. It was just something I did. It was something I had *always* done to escape my reality.

Now, something had changed. As I stood beside my father, looking about the room, I saw what he saw. Each rendering nearly glimmered as the light shone through the parchment reflecting a golden glow.

My father held up one image in particular. He held it up to his face, observing it closely. It was an image of Matilda, looking at her reflection in a lake, under the moonlight.

My face reddened as he examined it, and I suddenly felt transparent and foolish. Before I could explain myself, he smiled and looked at Father Caius.

"Yes, this will work. This will work *very* well," my father affirmed.

Father Caius nodded in agreement and stepped out of the room. My father followed suit, leaving me quite stupefied.

Before my father shut the door behind him, he turned to me, with a puzzled expression on his face.

"Where did you learn to draw like that?"

"I had hoped it was something I inherited from my father," I said, slightly prying into his mysterious past.

My father lifted his hands, which were slightly calloused and scarred.

"These hands repair watches, nothing more," he smiled.

"My hands repair watches, too," I said, taking two steps forward. Most of my years were spent in the old watch shop, just like my father. I wanted, so desperately, for him to know it. He shook his head, however, and took one final look around the room.

"But they could do so much more," he spoke faintly, and then he left.

Astonished, I was left to wonder what my father had seen in seconds, that I had taken *years* to see.

Chapter Four
A Great Necessity

"Look at the person beside you, for they will be your closest confidant on that momentous day," Father Caius spoke to us from the altar. Each of us sat on the benches looking at our surroundings with doubt.

Father Caius spent the previous day swearing the others to secrecy, as he showed them the beauty locked in the wardrobe.

"If we are to be united, we must place our faith wholly in each other," the old man said, looking at each one of us.

Although Father Caius was a wise man, I worried that he might have been too trusting. Could we trust Birch and Gideon? I wasn't sure, and I had only known them for a brief time. His faith in them, however, was unwavering, and I knew to trust the old priest's judgment.

Since witnessing the magic herself, Valentina walked around the church sighing blissfully everywhere she went. It was as though she was living in the greatest reverie.

"Isn't it *miraculous*?" She asked me, and I smiled.

Having Valentina in our circle would only make us stronger, I thought. Not only would her talents as a sculptress and artist prove useful, but her selfless optimism radiated any room. She was active and often vocal in her beliefs, and I had since considered her a good friend.

As we looked about the church at our small army, I was becoming quickly uplifted. When it came to soldiers, Larouche may have had numbers in his favor, but we had *integrity* in ours.

"For the record, I'd be happy dying beside each and every one of you," Patch began, "I'd be even happier if we went down like iron clad angels fighting for what we believe in … *armed and ready*."

A few of us rolled our eyes. I knew Patch welcomed Death and feared it not. It was why he sought open warfare and considered it the greatest cowardice to fall without so much as a fight.

"I just don't feel as though barging into the hotel with open fire is the right way to go about this," I interjected.

Patch stood up and handed each one of us a single piece of parchment paper with a map of the Hotel Larouche on it.

He then proceeded as though he were some skilled military general who would lead his troops into battle. He pointed out the secret entrances, and indefinite movements made by any guard at any given time.

The ideas all sounded irrational and far fetched. With an army of seven, it would be impossible to execute them artfully. Although Patch was my friend, I still felt it my duty to discourage any plans that could lead to tragedy.

"We've made it. We're in the hotel....*now what?*" Andrew baited Patch.

"We find the canvas," Patch responded simply.

"We could be searching for hours…*days*, even. You know Larouche's men. They'll fight to the death for him," my father pointed out.

"We need leverage," I spoke up. "We need to find someone who knows the hotel. A waiter maybe, or a bellboy…"

"So what do you propose we do then, *fierce leader*? Kidnap *Harvey Nicholas*, himself?" Patch scoffed.

Immediately, the room fell quiet. My breath quickened as I felt that we had somehow found a solution.

"*Absolutely.*"

Chatter arose instantly, as the energy in the room shifted from hopelessness to possibility. *Why not kidnap the man closest to the canvas?* A master manipulator, he could give us *all* the answers.

"You're ridiculous! It can't be done!" Patch jeered. "Some battles are best fought with a revolver."

"And some with the *mind*," I retorted. "I can't help but think that we have an easier way of distracting the patrons that raiding them. We need to create unease. With Harvey Nicholas gone, who knows what would happen!"

"How do you suggest we do that, Andrew?"

Father Caius, who had remained silent, spoke up.

"Honestly, I don't know, but it's a start. What would make Larouche more nervous than to have Harvey Nicholas gone? All his secrets would become undone, and his patrons would start to lose faith in him."

"It's an excellent idea, Andrew, but to kidnap him would be just as difficult as stealing the canvas itself!" Father Caius concluded.

"Exactly! Cut out the middle man and storm the hotel! It's the only way," Patch insisted, as he stood up.

"Let me see if I can scrounge up any shotguns or pistols …" he said, as he walked out of the room.

Valentina and I looked at each other and sighed. There would be no convincing him.

"Patch is a fighting man," Father Caius told the room. "The Hotel Larouche *molded* him that way. You'll have to imagine that there will be plenty of others who think as he does." Father Caius cautioned.

"Just a minute," my father said, sitting up in his seat on the bench. "Harvey Nicholas leaves the hotel frequently. I'd noticed it before on my route to retrieve medicine for Anais. Harvey often took a carriage *somewhere*," my father reminisced.

"Might you remember the *day*, Alben?" Father Caius pressed, as we all sat on the edge of our seats.

"I can't say I do, sadly. All your days tend to blur into the other at Larouche," he said, and I nodded in agreement.

"Not only when he left, but why?" Valentina spoke up. She was right. Why would Harvey have reason to leave the hotel?

"He always came back with a black bag," my father recalled, and each of us perked up a bit.

"A purchase, perhaps?" Birch interjected.

We all sat still in the church, each racking our brains for the one thing a magical canvas, which created everything, could *not* provide.

What could a man in want of nothing possibly need? There was no use for money. There was no use for sustenance and water. The canvas could replicate delicacies and jewels from all over the world … all you needed was a brush. A brush and some-

"Paint-"

Looking beside me, I noticed Patch who had re-entered the room, breathless. We had both spoken the possible answer to what we believed was the reason for Harvey's frequent departure at the same time.

"I saw him once in the Social Hour. He didn't frequent the place very often - a little to below his taste if you ask me. However, he came in and had a drink. I remember it well," Patch recalled.

"He looked unlike himself. His hair was askew and his glasses here tilted down on the bridge of his nose. I sensed something was wrong but sat observant regardless. He never mixes with the patrons, you see.

That's when Ol' Lox asked him what was in the bag he carried close to him. Harvey scoffed, and said 'If I told you it was a bag of paint - would you believe me?'"

We all smiled, as we realized that we suddenly had a *destination*.

"I thought it an odd answer then, but brushed it off as nothing more than Harvey being the ever mysterious crony he always was. Never liked him much myself," he ended.

"He's our way in," I said to Father Caius, and the old priest nodded in agreement.

"Then I will hold you and Patch in charge of his kidnapping," Father Caius commanded. We both looked at each other, and Patch grinned.

"With pleasure!" He chuckled and shook me by the shoulders. Suddenly, he looked alive again, as if he had a purpose. My role in all this would be to make sure Patch came back with Harvey Nicholas *alive*.

"Andrew, I feel great!" Patch said hours later, strutting around the room, clearly incapable of containing his enthusiasm. "When we capture that son of a bitch, I'll make sure he gives us all the answers we need."

"Patch ..." I began, but his excitement overpowered me. Once he settled down, he sat on the bed. I could see that he had something to say.

"What is it?" I asked.

"It's been a while since I've felt, well, *useful*. You spend your life being pushed away by the same woman - it does things to you. I was beginning to feel like there was no point to my existence. Yesterday, though, helping your sister ... I haven't done that in years!" he laughed, marveling at his hands in the air above him.

"These hands, here," he said, holding them out to me, "they don't just hold liquor and cigars, Andrew. They heal people! I'd nearly forgotten what a brilliant bastard I am!" he howled and flopped onto his bed. Then, he shot back up with a grin.

"You should have seen me in there. It was just like before! If only Tansy-"

He stopped short, then he stood up and peered out the window. Beside him, on its stand, stood the telescope pointed toward the night sky.

"You know something, Andrew? When you look at the moon, it's just an object, isn't it?" He looked through the telescope, pointing it toward the moon, then stood back up.

"But when you look closer and magnify it, you find so much more. That's how people are. We're no different, really."

The hurt Patch carried with him had not yet dissipated, and it probably never would. With time, however, I felt it could get better. He perked up slightly.

"Who knows what this canvas can bring!"

The statement hung in the air. There was so much to the canvas that we had not yet discovered, and I believed that Patch chased it hoping it would lead to some kind of happiness for him. I suppose we all felt that in some way. We all toyed with the possibilities the canvas had in store for us, though I wouldn't let myself get lost in it.

Matilda's memory still stung whenever she crossed my mind. I feared it was growing worse when most nights, consumed with guilt, I discovered that not even sleep could comfort me.

That night I crawled into bed, ready to spend eight hours staring at the ceiling as I often did. To my surprise, however, my eyelids grew heavy until they rested entirely over my eyes. This was about to become the deepest slumber of my life.

That night my dreams played out a familiar scene. It was a dream I had had before and one that nearly suffocated my mind ever since.

I found myself in a familiar little chapel, faced with Father Caius. Once again, we walked toward each other slowly. He descended from the altar as though he had been expecting me for some time. As I desperately willed my legs to cease their steps, I heard large doors shut behind me. Why, I thought, was this happening to me again?

At last, we met in the center of the church, and Father Caius turned toward the right, slowly.

My body betrayed me as I, too, turned in the same direction as Father Caius.

There they were. The confessionals stood a few paces from us, and I knew what we were about to do.

Both of us walked toward the curtains in what may have been the most excruciating journey. Only darkness awaited me there. There was no more light.

"I've been here before, Father. Why are you doing this to me?" I half whispered, inwardly cursing at myself for continuing our walk to what was perhaps my impending doom.

He didn't respond, but in his silence hung such a heaviness. Describing such a feeling was impossible.

When at last we were in the confessionals, I collapsed down onto my knees, my breaths shortening as every second went by.

The chilled voice spoke at last.

"What is Andrew Godfrey's greatest fear?" Father Caius said. The words were unwelcome, as I revisited them in my mind over and over again. This time, however, I had an answer.

"Matilda," I muttered, and the window creaked open slowly. "I fear losing Matilda for good. I fear never being able to love again."

Upon my last words, the window had opened entirely. My heart leapt as I realized that Matilda was sitting across from me.

"Matilda! Matilda, can you hear me?" I shouted, banging the meshed iron gate with my fists.

She couldn't, I realized, and before I could call out to her again, I noticed something all too terrifying. Matilda's flesh began to rot. Her skin turned grey as her eyes sank into her skull.

Quickly, I stood up and stumbled away from her. The heat had returned with a vengeance.

Without looking, I saw what my fate was to be. The flames had come back for me once again.

This time was different, however. Instead of trying to run from the fire below, I closed my eyes and allowed myself to fall.

Chapter Five
The Caravan

Underneath the cloudless sky, Patch and I rode away from the church on our horses, ready to begin our unnerving quest as we followed the Maven, himself.

Each one of us carried a satchel with our rations. In our pockets, we each kept a small pocket knife for protection, though I doubt I'd know how to use it should such an occasion come.

Along with some blankets and rope, we carried a knapsack with what was necessary.

We were less than a mile out when Patch and I were able to spot a small town in the distance. It looked no different from my hometown, Howell Village. The dwellings and shops were both grim looking and small.

Like Howell, this place was built for necessity and nothing more. Even its scent was familiar, with its wet stone floors and its rotted wooden porches. This place smelled like it had been long forgotten. If I closed my eyes, it would be no different from Howell at all.

We pulled up to a post and tied our horses to it. A few passersby regarded us briefly before continuing whatever consumed them previously.

Besides the post was a crooked and withered looking sign that read 'Quagmire Street'.

So this was Quagmire. I'd often hear about our neighbors as a boy. Their advancements in light and the evolution of the candle to the gaslight had been the talk of our town. Howell Residents often moved here in the hopes of bettering their lives and joining a more forward thinking community.

From the looks of things, however, they hadn't moved that much ahead.

"I can't say I miss this," Patch said. "Although, life at the church isn't something I fancy either."

As soon as the horses were tied up, we made our way down the cobblestone street, with some apprehension. Most places held some secrets, and I wondered what Quagmire might have been concealing.

"Come, Andrew," Patch called out. He was heading toward a small shop along the left side of the street. A large sign that read 'Porter's General Store' hung over the storefront. We had made it.

"Now, I will have to tell you, that shovel isn't nearly as effective as this one. See the angles on it. That's fine craftsmanship right there."

In the shop, a scruffy looking man with a round face was speaking jovially to an older fellow. Wearing a workers apron, he stood behind the counter holding two shovels, weighing their differences with his arms like a human scale.

"Alright then, Mr. Porter. I'll take it," The older gentleman sighed. He realized that he had been swindled, as he shook his head and took out a few bills from his jacket pocket.

The man at the counter smiled triumphantly, and then suddenly became aware of the fact that he had *two more* customers in his store.

"I'll be with you two in a moment," he called out, and Patch waved him off, carefully examining a pair of women's slippers.

"How would I look in these?" he asked me, and I smiled. He certainly knew how to make light of any situation.

"Right, gentleman," Mr. Porter called out, as the older gentleman left the store. The shopkeeper stood alert and wide-eyed, as though he had discovered a well in the middle of the desert. Little did he realize, we hadn't a cent to our names.

"How may I assist you?" He beamed. Patch took no notice of his enthusiasm.

"We'd like some paint," Patch said, resting his hand on the counter. The man's excitement deflated slightly, before remembering that a purchase was *still* a purchase.

He hurried over to a neatly stacked pile of paint cans and held out his arms.

"Take as many as you like, gentleman!" He nearly sang, but Patch merely shook his head in response.

"Paint for a *canvas*, not a *fence*."

The smile on the rotund man's face faded quickly. With great exasperation, he sighed, "I'm afraid we have none!"

Patch looked at me as if he could scarcely believe it. This *small convenience store couldn't* be the location we thought Mr.Nicholas purchased his paint from … or *could i*t?

Atop a shelf, behind the greedy shopkeeper, sat a set of acrylics neatly piled in sort of pyramid formation. He had *lied*. Quickly, I looked at Patch to see if he had noticed the paints, but he hadn't.

"Are those not for sale?" I asked, pointing at the paint. Patch instantly followed my finger and crossed his arms.

"Well, look at that! You have paints after all!" He spoke out, sarcastically.

"I can't sell those to you, gentlemen. The man who buys them from me pays twice what they're worth so that I can keep them in stock for him. Peculiar man, too! I think he's a bit of a hermit."

Patch and I both looked at each other, each trying with much difficulty to contain our excitement. Harvey Nicholas was within our grasp and, soon, he'd be a pawn in this game we were playing.

"When will he be in again? Perhaps my friend and I could purchase them from *him*?" I suggested, slyly. The man thought about my question for a moment.

"Well, let's see. It's Tuesday … so, he should be in tomorrow - he likes coming in here on Wednesdays. He'll probably be here early in the morning."

"Excellent," I said, my voice barely coming out in a whisper. The plan was coming together *beautifully.* I could hardly believe it.

Patch and I both looked at each other knowingly. We had gotten the information we needed and would be back again the next morning, with shackles for our *new guest*.

Before we could make our way out of the shop, Mr. Porter leaned in close.

"I've never see you two before. From where do you hail? From the looks of it," he eyed us, then continued, "you both look like you're not from around here." His eyes squinted with all sorts of speculation.

"Have you heard of the Hotel Larouche friend?" Patch asked, leaning in close. The man's eyebrows lifted, as he whispered.

"*I thought so!*" he said, his mouth watering slightly. The distant thought of the Hotel Larouche, like any man, was not far from his thoughts. He leaned in closer, eager for a word about the place, so overcome by its mystique. "What is it *like*?"

Patch looked at me and shook his head. To honestly describe the hotel in its entirety would take more than just a word from a stranger. I sensed Patch didn't want to divulge in it any longer. Instead, he left with a single phrase.

"It's what dreams are made made of, *friend*. And *nightmares*."

We left the shop, tipping our hats on the way out. Patch threw a glance my way, and I sensed that he was somewhat proud of our feat back in the old shop. Harvey

Nicholas was within our reach and tomorrow, we would have all the answers we needed.

***

After a stop at a local inn for some supper, we took our leave and made our way to the woods. Our resting place for the night was to be nothing more elegant than the crook of a tree underneath our thin blankets. I had never spent the night outside before, with nothing more than a barn owl and some June bugs for companionship.

Patch, on the other hand, appeared as though he were no stranger to the primitive lifestyle. He settled into a tree's divot with ease and placed his hands behind his head comfortably.

"There have been many men slain in woods like these," Patch said, as he closed his eyes.

"What's wrong with you?" I asked, looking over my shoulders, and he chuckled.

"Leading people, Andrew, is simply fooling them into believing you know what you're doing. You've never slept a night out like this, have you?" He asked as he opened his eyes. I shook my head.

"Is it that obvious?"

Patch closed his eyes again, when - all at once - a drum sounded not too far from where we had camped out. Patch and I both hopped to our feet, breathless.

"Let's get a closer look!" Patch said. Grabbing our belongings, we made our way slowly toward the direction of the sound. "Better we find them before they find us."

Slowly, we crept closer and closer to the flames burning in the dead of night. A small caravan of wanderers was chanting and drinking from clay cups. Not far from them sat an old mare attached to a painted wagon.

Laughter and howls filled the air around them, as the man with the drum played a lively beat. One woman stood out, as she began to coordinate her movements to the rhythm. Her arms floated above her head, as she spun around in a circle, her layered skirt moving gently with the wind. The others in the group all clapped in unison as encouragement while she continued to dance. Then, in one swift action, she removed the scarf from her hair, sending an abundance of curly magenta waves falling to her shoulders.

A twig beneath Patch's foot snapped, as he took a step forward. The sound of the drum ceased immediately, and we were all left staring at the dancer who had suddenly stopped her swaying.

"*Patch!*" The woman gasped. The circle of six all turned their heads toward the two intruders who had spoiled their fun. Immediately, a tall man with shoulder length hair stood up beside her.

"Do you know this man?" He asked, and she nodded.

"This man is a phantom. He *must* be. The man I remember would never leave the Hotel Larouche," she spoke, as she walked toward him.

Anxiously, I looked at Patch, whose face was rigid and stern. Before him stood Tansy, the woman he loved and pined after for so long and, yet, he could say *nothing.* Instead, he turned around swiftly and headed back to our spot in the woods.

"Patch!" Tansy called out; then she noticed me still standing there in the dark. Before she could speak, I turned back into the woods and followed my friend. There was much on his mind, to be sure.

Upon my arrival at the campfire, I came to a halt - breathless and worried. I relaxed, when I noticed Patch, standing against a tree, smoking. With one hand in his pocket, his gaze fell to the floor, lost in thought. It was as though he were trying to decide if Tansy's appearance in the woods was a good or bad thing. In truth, I felt the same way.

Tansy had been the sole source of pain for my friend, but the tension between them could also have been attributed to the hotel itself. No relationship or connection of love could bloom there. Nothing, not even a flower could survive in such a place. If given a second chance, away from the hotel, perhaps things would turn out better.

"I thought I'd feel differently when I saw her again. I thought I'd feel angry, Andrew, but I don't. I feel just as I used to," he scoffed, taking another puff from his cigarette.

A soft rustle came from behind me. I turned to see Tansy, with a shawl wrapped around her shoulders, emerge through the shadows.

"What are you two doing out here?" She asked us. "It's dangerous. Larouche has men scanning the villages for you, Andrew. They raided our caravan just a few days ago."

"We're fine," I assured her. "We're leaving tomorrow."

"What trouble have you gotten yourself into now, Patch?" She asked, but Patch merely rolled his eyes.

"Now that's none of your business, is it?" He replied, hotly. She looked at him, her lips trembling slightly, before turning back to me.

"Be safe, Andrew," She said, grabbing my hand, an action not lost on Patch. Then she turned back to her former lover and crossed her arms.

"I must say I'm surprised to see you away from the hotel, Patch. I hoped that it had changed you for good, but I can see that it *hasn't*. Goodnight, gentleman." She ended, retreating into the forest.

Patch watched her go, craning his neck slightly. He then rolled up his sleeves and took a seat on the forest floor, clearly agitated. After a moment, I noticed him force himself to relax, as he nestled in between the grooves of the tree. With a long sigh, he took one last puff of his cigarette.

"I thought you still had feelings for her," I mentioned casually, as I pulled a blanket over my legs.

"I do, but I'll not give her the satisfaction of thinking so *ever* again."

Chapter Six
Waiting

I had already prepared the horses when Patch awoke the next morning. He sat awhile, possibly wondering if the night before had been a scene from his dreams. After a moment, he looked over his shoulder, lost in thought.

"We're all set," I told him, placing the blankets on my horse. They were still tied to the trees and would stay there until we had come back with Harvey.

My satchel around me, I stood with my arms crossed, looking down at my lovestruck cohort.

"Alright then," he said, as he brought himself to his feet. I could sense that he was unnerved. Tansy's appearance the night before had caused him to lose sight of himself, and the task he had set out accomplish.

We made our way over to the outskirts of the little town, keeping a close watch on all those who both entered and departed. At nearly six in the morning, not too many people were about. Still, I knew that quiet mornings often masked wild and emphatic evenings.

One hour passed, and then another. We sat perched just behind the side of the general store, waiting.

At eight in the morning, Patch and I grew restless. My hands loosened their grip on the shackles I held. Patch took out a set of binoculars he had brought with him and held them up to his eyes, desperately searching the plains for any sign of our prey.

"Where is he?" Patch whispered to no one in particular.

"He's probably indulging in the hot cuisine back at the hotel," I sulked, and my stomach nearly grumbled in response.

"Yes, while I'm stuck out here with you," Patch replied. "Remind me why I'm here again?"

"Because, for once in your life you're doing something that may, in fact, better mankind."

"Oh, right," Patch said, putting the binoculars down. "The *betterment of mankind* doesn't seem quite worth it when you're hungry."

We must have sat there for another hour, watching the sun emerge.

If Harvey knew what awaited him he would not be pleased. *Who was Harvey Nicholas?* I asked myself. What sort of life did he lead, as assistant to his revered master Meir Larouche?

"Andrew," Patch whispered, "He's coming ... and he's *not* alone."

Patch handed me the binoculars, and I quickly took them. When I peered through them, I noted that Harvey was guarded by two men, possibly the same men that were searching for us at the old church.

"Hold this, Andrew." Patch said, handing me a revolver.

"Patch, what are you doing with this?" I asked, as I tucked the gun away beneath my shirt.

"*For the betterment of mankind,* Andrew," he teased. "Only use it if all else fails," he ordered, and then he mumbled slightly under his breath, "Just don't blow your damn hand off."

We pushed ourselves up against the wall of the shop and steadied our breath. At once, the horses came to a full stop, then boots hit the dirt road and climbed the creaking steps.

"Wait here, gentleman," one voice commanded. The bell from the shop rang, as the shopkeeper greeted the guest.

"Well now, I've been expecting you!" He said, just before the door shut. Patch and I looked at each other knowingly. The time had come, and there was no turning back now.

"Keep your hand on that revolver, Andrew. We may have to use it soon."

"Or not," I responded, looking at the back end of the shop. I had remembered something from the previous day, something that I had noticed on my way out of the general store.

Quickly, I crept away from the porch, Patch's frantic whispers sounding behind me. "What are you doing? Stick to the plan, Andrew!" He hissed.

With determination, I reached the end of the left side of the shop and turned immediately. There it was, a back window. *Another way in.*

The window wasn't so high up that I couldn't climb in, so I pushed it open slightly, praying to enter the shop undetected. With a bit of a jump, I lifted myself in and stepped down into the shop landing right behind the same pyramid of paint cans that the shopkeeper had tried to sell us the day before.

My steps were light, as I moved around the paint cans slowly. Apart from the three of us, the shop was empty.

The shopkeeper was boisterously talking to his prized customer.

The time is now, Andrew Godfrey, I thought. *Be brave.*

"Harvey Nicholas," I spoke, trying to steady my voice that quivered slightly.

Harvey stood still at first, then turned around slowly. His eyes met my own and his lips spread into a thin smile. It was as if he had been expecting me.

"This is the man, Mr. Nicholas! He and his friend were inquiring about the paint I keep aside for you…"

"Quiet," Harvey said, cutting off the shopkeeper, who immediately ceased his introduction.

At no point did Harvey remove his eyes from me. It was as though he was mentally predicting my every move and I had to admit that it was making me uneasy.

"You're going to want to come with me," I warned him. The shopkeeper, in his confusion, looked back and forth at the two of us. Harvey merely leaned against the counter, challengingly.

"Is that right?" He asked.

"We can make this very easy, Mr. Nicholas. There doesn't have to be any discord if you come with me."

Nicholas still didn't move but looked on the way that a spectator at the circus did. He saw me as a child and no real threat whatsoever.

Without thinking, I drew my gun out in front of me. The shopkeeper gasped and shrank back in fear. In truth, I didn't even know how to use it, as I had never had to use one before. All that I relied on was the significant intimidation that it provided.

"Are you going to shoot me, Andrew Godfrey?" He asked, candidly. It was as though he had brushed my threat aside, clearly unaffected.

"I don't want to, but I will do what needs to be done," I gulped. *What was I saying?*

"Andrew Godfrey, the boy everyone is looking for. The one who chose to be so defiant is now headhunted like a murder. You started a war, Andrew Godfrey. Larouche won't stop until he bears witness to your final breath."

"*Me?*" I asked, in disbelief. "I don't understand."

Harvey Nicholas took a few steps toward me until, at last, his chest was inches from my the barrel of my revolver. Under his breath, he whispered so that only I could hear him.

"The only thing worse than a *war* is the person who caused it."

Harvey proceeded to step around me as he maneuvered out of the window, while I stood there, quite stunned with the architect's reproach.

With my pistol still aimed at him, I turned to the shopkeeper.

"*You!* Get in that room and close the door!" I ordered, and I watched the man cower in fear as he ran to the small storage room. Immediately, I followed Harvey out of the window to find Patch awaiting us with a wide grin.

"Hello, Harvey!" He nearly sang, grabbing the bag of paint from our prisoner. Harvey unwillingly relinquished it.

"We don't have much time," I interjected, placing the shackles around Harvey's wrists.

"Is that really necessary?" He asked, dryly.

Neither of us responded to his question, as we hastily locked the shackles. We didn't have long before Harvey's companions discovered what had happened.

We bounded into the woods, dragging our prisoner with us as we went. Our horses were but a few yards away. After a moment, a single shot blasted behind us. Frantically, I approached our small campground, desperately trying to gather our belongings.

"It's too late, Andrew! This way!" Patch whispered from a few yards ahead. Quickly, we followed him, hearing the booming sound of two more gunshots behind us. This time, two loud thuds resounded. The forest floor shook slightly, as I realized the sound came from our horses being shot down. It was evident to me that these beasts, Larouche's men, would stop at nothing.

In my anger, I began to head back when Patch called out to me.

"Do not make this easy for them, Andrew," he warned.

Together, we all made our way toward a river bank. Harvey and I stood, out of breath, watching Patch as he dove into the icy cold water. With some trepidation, I knew that jumping in was the only option.

With the two guards behind us, there was no time to think. A moment longer, and we would be discovered! We all stood in the water and took in one final gasp of air before we sank back into the muddy river.

They must have arrived at the edge of the bank. In the distance, I noticed Harvey try to move closer to the surface. Quickly, I swam toward him, using the towering rock formations to conceal my movements. In a moment, I pinned him down, the crashing waves providing the perfect curtain of concealment. Our brutish consorts looked up and down the river. Silently, I prayed that they'd leave before my hand, still covering Harvey's mouth, muted his life forever.

Finally, as if God *himself* had been watching, the men left, grunting as they went. Breathless, I released my grip on Harvey who gasped for air.

Quickly, I pulled him up to the surface and dragged his weak body toward the nook of a tree.

"That was unpleasant," Patch said, rising out of the water and ringing out the ends of his shirt.

"What now," Harvey satirized, and Patch and I looked at each other. With no horses, it would be at least a day's walk, and Larouche's men were undoubtedly already on their way back to their master. Larouche would come for us himself if it meant that he would retrieve his precious lackey. We had gotten ourselves into something much bigger than any of us could imagine.

"I think you'll be needing some horses, then," a soft voice spoke.

We all looked toward where the voice had come from and found Tansy, standing beside a horse of her own.

Nothing was turning out how we had expected it to, but from the way Patch regarded his former mistress … he didn't mind that one bit.

Chapter Seven
Journey Home

It was nearly two o' clock when the caravan decided to rest for a bite to eat. Patch and I each rode a horse, while Harvey sat in the wagon, carefully observant of his surroundings. It was as though he were looking at the outside world for the first time. He hadn't spoken a word since we'd left the small town.

We all sat, like gypsies, deep in the towering blades of grass and ate a simple meal comprised of bread and jam.

Neither Patch nor Tansy spoke to one another, making it the most unbearable silences I'd been a part of in some time.

"So, what's he doing here? A bit odd isn't it?" Tansy asked me, motioning over toward Harvey.

"It's a long story," I sighed. Tansy looked at me, cocking her eyebrow as though she was displeased with my answer.

"Yes, well, it's a free ride so…" she smiled.

Nervously, I looked at Patch, who looked back at me. Could we include Tansy into our little secret? It felt wrong to tell her without asking the others first.

"You should come back with us then," I suggested. Patch choked back a piece of his bread.

"What, you mean to stay with you?" She asked, and I nodded. Then she shook her head and threw a quick look at Patch.

"I couldn't do that," She said, possibly rejecting the idea that the two of them living under the same roof again could be a good thing.

"That's too bad. We're going to change the world," I said, with confidence, but Tansy merely laughed in response.

"You got a strange group for that, don't you think?" She said, rolling her eyes toward Patch. Then she leaned in and whispered, "Although, you did manage to get him to leave that old place, so I guess I should believe you. Miracles *are* possible!" She jeered, and Patch threw his bread down on the floor.

"Andrew, we're wasting time. We should go," he said, clearly avoiding Tansy's critical eyes.

"Would you care to ride my horse?" I asked Tansy, who had been sharing a horse with another member of the group. Patch whipped his head around with wide eyes. Quickly, I explained myself.

"It's just that I'd like to sit in the wagon for a bit."

Patch relaxed, and Tansy instantly agreed. I wondered if she saw it as an opportunity to have some time alone with her old friend.

As we all resumed our journey, I climbed my way up the wagon and perched down directly in front of Harvey.

"Lost?" He asked.

"I'm sorry it had to be this way, Harvey. You're just on the wrong side is all," I shrugged. Something about him made me believe that there was much more to him than a person could see at first glance.

"Wrong side? There is no wrong side, Andrew." He stated it naturally, as though he genuinely believed it.

"Of course there is … "

"Why are you here, Andrew? What are you searching for? Because if you're looking for what I think you're looking for, know this; There will never be a *wrong* side," he spoke boldly.

"But ... why?" I asked, and Harvey settled into his seat with a sigh. In a whisper, he spoke.

"As long as it exists, someone will always be its possessor. Good intentions or not, eventually it's used for selfish reasons. No man or woman can resist its temptations."

"I don't believe that. We are human beings, not animals. We have laws to govern us, a moral compass, and minds capable of creating good," I stated with passion, but Harvey waved me off.

"No one is capable of just that, Andrew, trust me. You'll see that in a day or two," he concluded, but I couldn't rest.

"What do you *mean*?"

"Did you not consider that once Larouche discovers your careless rouse, he'll come for you? You must return me to him before they begin to notice," he said, looking at the outstretched land before him. "Things could fall apart fast at the hotel without me. It could be a matter of days. Larouche would face a threat much greater than you," he paused, looking me straight in the eyes as if he was trusting me with vital information.

"The hotel, everything in it would unravel, and Larouche's secret would be out. The patrons would eventually see reality, and all would be lost."

Harvey looked around at our fellow travelers as if he had just spoken words that could lead to his undoing

"Why should I believe you? You have loyalty to nothing and *no one*," I asked, speculatively.

"It's true, Andrew. I have no loyalty to any one person in particular, but I *do* have loyalty to the canvas. It's all I know, and I will fight and die to protect it."

"So, it does really work then?" I asked, curiously.

"If you don't believe in it, what in Hell's name are you chasing after?" Harvey asked, incredulously.

"I dunno. I have my doubts, like anyone."

"Doubts are only for those who are weak of character, Andrew," Harvey responded, and I gulped. Harvey, I noted, was full of conviction, and made little room for any sort of fickleness.

"Still, it seems so … miraculous. My mind can't imagine it happening."

"That is because your mind is small and incapable of comprehending such things. You were raised in Howell Village after all."

"Thank you?" I responded, slightly wounded.

"Expand, Andrew. Always keep the mind expanding. Dream up inconceivable things, *always*."

Our little conversation was over, but it had left me wondering if Harvey's words held any truth in them. The patrons of the hotel had been so long lost in the misted facade that they needed to see their world crumble to realize that it was but a dream all along.

Settling into my spot on the wagon, I pulled out my sketchbook and pencils and began to draw. Frequently, I noticed Harvey taking an interest in what I was drawing. At first, I sketched the front porch of my home back in Howell Village, detailing in the uneven planks and chipped paint.

After that was completed, I placed a figure seated on a bench. Halfway through, I realized this person was Matilda, as I always wanted to see her.

As I continued drawing, my mind began to wander to a short memory I had of Matilda from a few years back.

The sun had just started to set as I was tending to our garden. On my knees, I felt sweat trickle down my neck, as I raked through the dirt with my hands. So lost in my daydreams, I didn't even realize that Matilda Brew had approached our house.

"Godfrey, please stop what you are doing to see my newest discovery." She said, barging through the gate.

Taken aback, I instantly stood up and dusted myself off. She didn't need to ask twice, as I removed my gloves and tossed them on the grass.

"Wh-what is it?" I asked, nervously.

As if unveiling the rarest of treasures, Matilda opened her hand to reveal a small wheel like object. It rotated in all directions. I had never seen anything like it before.

"It's a *gyroscope*," she responded, and I looked at it, perplexed.

"Based on the Earth's gravity, it can determine orientation," she said, holding it closer to me.

We made our way up the porch steps and sat on the bench. As we fell into the cushions, a small cloud of dust lifted off the seat. Everything we owned was dust-ridden and rotted through, it seemed.

Matilda, so lost in the gyroscope, didn't seem to notice.

"Where did you find it?" I asked as she handed it to me.

"My father gave it to me," she began. "He said it reminded him of his oldest daughter."

I had to admit that I couldn't understand the similarity her father had discovered in the object and his

Matilda. What did he mean by comparing the two? As in answer to my thoughts, Matilda responded.

"He said that I spent life going around as if I had swallowed a gyroscope. As though I was continually moving in any direction with no constant plans ahead of me. He said it's an excellent way to live."

Smiling, I nodded in agreement.

"It is!"

"I always thought that not having plans meant you weren't really going anywhere, but I have plans to go to Paris and India and so many other places!"

"It just means that you're prepared for anything that comes your way. Anything."

She smiled back at me and nudged me slightly.

"Do you really think so?" She asked, leaning close.

Before I could respond, something caught my eye, something that I hadn't noticed before. Dangling beneath her cream-colored dress was something black. Her dress drifted moved up slightly to reveal a *black hoof.*

Terrified, I had closed my sketchbook and was instantly transported out of the dream and back to my seat on the wagon. Harvey looked over to me as I tried to settle my breathing.

Why had my mind conjured up such damnable images? I had remembered once, my mother telling us that a black goat was a symbol of *bad luck*. Perhaps the hoof I saw was its representation in Matilda's life. Her aspirations would end at the moment of her death. Alternatively, maybe the whole memory was riddled with the guilt I felt over Matilda.

I couldn't be sure. As I looked across at Harvey Nicholas, I saw him smiling at me as if he knew things that I couldn't possibly imagine. *What had I done?* I thought.

Most importantly, what was I prepared to do?

Chapter Eight
Winding Hours

"That's your brilliant plan? Become his *apprentice?*" Patch shouted.

We had just arrived after a three hour journey across the deserted plains. Father Caius and Valentina were seated in the sacristy while Harvey had been taken to the cellar. He was locked in, far removed from any sunlight.

We had barely settled in when Patch demanded that we construct a plan immediately. He was right about one thing. Word of Harvey's disappearance would reach Larouche's ears soon enough, and we had less than a day to decide what was needed.

When I revealed my plan to the others, Patch rose from his seat instantly. His eyes widened as he looked to the others for support.

"I can't be the only one who sees what's wrong with this picture, can I? We have the maven, so now what? You want us to *learn* from him? We don't have the time!" he spat.

"What did you expect?" I asked. Patch lifted his arms in the air.

"Revolution! He's a pawn, Andrew, and our way in! We should march over there now, baring arms with every man and woman who will join us."

"We can't. Not yet."

Father Caius spoke up as he placed his hand on the table, deeply contemplating his next decision.

"Andrew's right. Our job will be much easier if we catch the patrons at a vulnerable moment. Let them feel uneasy. Let them wake up from their reveries shaken. That is when Larouche will be at his weakest."

Patch threw his arms over his head with defeat. We seemed to always be in some disagreement lately.

In frustration, he made his way out of the room. Just before he left, however, he nudged me on his way out and I followed him.

"I'll have you know I'm not happy we're inviting *her* to stay here," he scoffed. "It's not your decision to make."

In my foolishness, I had invited Tansy to join us and take a break from her life migrating with a traveling caravan. To my surprise, she agreed! Valentina decided that they would share an old room once occupied by one of the long deceased monks from the old monastery.

Patch, of course, agreed with *none* of this.

"It's not *yours* either." I reminded him. "It's hers."

Patch looked at me, challengingly, before he pushed me into the stone wall.

"Stay out of my affairs, Andrew, or you'll have another enemy on your hands."

He walked away, not saying anymore, leaving me stunned and beside myself. The only thing I noticed was the liquor bottle sticking out of his back pocket.

Something was wrong with Patch, but as the minutes ticked by, I knew I didn't have the time to worry about it. *He could take care of himself*, I tried to convinced myself.

Only one day had passed, but I realized that I longed to see my family, my *sister* especially. Quickly, I ran up the stairs and opened the door to my sister's room.

I walked in to find Gideon laying strips of wet cloth along Anais's forehead. My father, who stood at the window, turned around and smiled.

"Andrew!" He beamed. It felt good to be welcomed in such a way. "I must have stayed awake all night, cursing myself for not going with you boys."

"It was nothing," I shrugged. "Harvey came with us almost *willingly*."

My father pondered this a minute and then nodded, pensively. "I've always thought that Larouche had an agenda, but Harvey Nicholas had his own. I wonder what he means by complying so easily."

My father was *right*. Somehow I felt that Harvey's allegiance was with himself and no one else. It seemed that the man was an *enigma*. I wanted to trust him but knew that I'd fall into a trap he'd been setting for me all along. Harvey was not a friend. He was an accomplice to a man of pure evil.

Father Caius entered the room, closing the door behind him. The expression he wore was a mixture of both delight and relief.

"I may have found the perfect opportunity for us," he revealed, gathering us around him.

My father and I looked at each other, apprehensively, as we wondered what news the old man had to share. The hours were dwindling by faster than we wanted them to, and we were short of a well constructed plan.

"There is a masquerade at the Hotel Larouche in *two* days. One of our clergy men had a horrid encounter with two of Larouche's men this morning. His carriage was upturned and raided earlier today. It seems that Larouche has been sending his men to conduct random checks of carriages lately. No one was hurt, by the grace of God, and the man and his family were safe. He did hear, however, one of the men talk about the upcoming celebration, mentioning that he needed to choose a mask soon."

Father Caius placed his hands on our shoulders.

"As in an act of God, *this* is our moment," he whispered and looked at me. "Andrew, tomorrow night I need you to leave here with the others and slowly make your way to the Hotel Larouche. We can't wait any longer or they will destroy the chapel and all of us with it, do you understand?"

"Yes," I responded without hesitation. "But where will you be?"

"I will show you tomorrow. The patrons need something to pull them from the darkness. We cannot win this if we don't prepare."

He walked back out of the room, checking in on Anais before he left. Gideon, my father, and I all looked at each other with the same thought in our mind.

In two days, one way or another, we'd be back at the hotel. Quickly, I followed the old man out of the room.

"Father Caius!" I shouted just as he was about to turn the corner.

In all this, there was something that didn't feel quite right, and I hoped the priest could make sense of it for me. He stopped when heard me calling and his eyebrows furrowed together.

"You look upset, Andrew. Is there something wrong?" Father Caius asked, and I nodded.

"Patch. He seems *different*," I responded truthfully, The priest placed his hands on the table.

"Patch feels out of place here, but that doesn't mean it's *not* where he belongs. He needs time to adjust and, in the meantime, he'll do what he can to feel like himself," Father Caius said in response to my concern and continued, "Patch has his doubts, like the rest of us. He just wears it differently."

"Doubt? In *me*?" I whispered, and Father Caius shook his head.

"*You*, Andrew? *Never*. You are the one piece of the puzzle that fits so perfectly in all this. You are a painter with a true lion's heart. You were meant to be here today! We are starting a revolution that only *you* can lead. Patch may not show it but he knows this to be true."

Admittedly, I was grateful to hear the old man's response, but I shuddered knowing that such a profound responsibility was left to me. As long as I had everyone's support, however, I hoped I could lead them with dignity.

I couldn't understand how everyone had put such faith in me. Who was *I* to merit such a position amongst the talented individuals that stood with me? It felt almost *wrong*. In my mind, I pictured the community back at Howell laughing at the thought of me, Andrew Godfrey, leading anyone!

The only time I felt sure of anything was when I was with Matilda, and she was *gone*. What else was left for me but the sketches I created as a means of dulling my senses. When the world felt as though it were crumbling around me, sketching *restored* it.

It was fortunate that I should find such an opportunity at hand. The canvas gave me new reason and a desire to take on the day. The more I thought about it, the more I felt a strange sort kinship for it. It was as though, many miles away, it was beckoning me to be its *protector*.

Standing in the empty hallway, I realized that there was only one thing left for me to do before the day came to an end.

It was time for my first lesson.

CHAPTER NINE
ALL IN THE DETAILS

In the depths of the cellar, I found him painting listlessly with a long, thin brush. Spectacles resting at the end of his nose, as he leaned closer to the parchment.

Father Caius thought it wise gather some art supplies for Harvey, so we could begin our lessons immediately. There was much I had to learn and we weren't certain of how much time we had to do so.

It was also a welcomed pastime for our mock prisoner who would spend the next day in solitude in our humble cellar. However, I felt as though Harvey didn't mind the seclusion. From the looks of things, he seemed to prefer it.

Quietly, I walked behind him and observed the landscape he was creating. The painting depicted an open field leading to a greater beyond. Each blade of grass held such realism, wilting as from a cool breeze on a summer's day. It was extraordinary and yet, so seemingly simple.

Harvey didn't acknowledge my presence. He looked at the canvas in front of him, so lost in his work that I couldn't find it in me to disturb him. At long last, he spoke.

"It's freeing … to paint something like this," he said, standing back a bit to admire his landscape. "Much less demanding than drawing the makings of a hotel every day."

Nodding, I took in the artist's appearance. He was slightly shorter than myself, and looked both intellectual and stern. His eyebrows came together as he looked at his creation, possibly searching for something *more* to add to it.

"Did you always want to paint?" I inquired. He instantly shook his head.

"*Never*. It was something I was good at when I was a boy. Everyone headed off to school in the morning, and I stayed back to paint portraits for the town officials and their wives. It was how I earned my keep," he recalled. "To be entirely honest, I hardly ever paint for pleasure. It's a luxury I can't afford."

"Will you teach me?" I asked hesitantly, and he looked at me with wide eyes.

"Not to paint. I know how to paint," I stammered. "I'd like to know how to use the canvas. How does it work?"

It was evident that he was thinking about his next step. Would it be wise to teach a stranger the particulars of his master's most guarded treasure? I imagined not, but his response surprised me. He removed the canvas from the easel and replaced it with another. Then, he turned to me and held out his brush.

"Go ahead. Give it a try," Harvey said, looking at me almost challengingly.

With some hesitation, I took the brush and held it in my hands, twisting it as I regarded small indents on the handle. The initials H. N. were carved into it.

"It's an ordinary brush. Nothing too spectacular about it," Harvey said.

Nodding, I returned my focus to the canvas before me. Never had an object intimidated me so. Taking Harvey's color palette in my left hand, I slowly dipped the brush into a daub of brown paint. Nervously, I brought my hand to the canvas, careful not to spill a single drop of paint.

As soon as the brush made contact with the canvas, the strokes and lines on the page became effortless. It was the most familiar feeling in the world. I had found my place of comfort as I painted the figure of a woman looking into a mirror. The woman was, of course, Matilda. It was a vision that I had seen before.

She was looking in a mirror, not realizing she would eventually come to *live* in it.

All the while, Harvey sat behind me with crossed arms, watching from a distance. When I placed the brush down, he stood up and walked to the portrait.

"Excellent work, Andrew," he said, without the smallest hint of satisfaction. It was as if he had expected it.

He looked at the picture and studied it for a while, suddenly making me very anxious.

"Now, suppose the woman needs fresh air. Paint a window," he commanded.

Finding his instruction peculiar, I drew a small box window beside the mirror. After I had completed painting in the window, he walked around to the other side and pointed to a spot next to the girl.

"She loves looking at the wallpaper. It reminds her of the striped walls at her grandmother's house. Give her something to look at."

Again, I dipped the brush in the paint and began constructing the vertically striped wall.

Wiping the sweat from my forehead, I turned to Harvey who looked beside the finished wall with a quizzical expression.

"She'll want to go the kitchen, won't she?" he asked. "Paint a door that leads her there."

After his third command, I began to grow irritated as I couldn't place a reason for them. Quickly, I drew a door with a knob and stood back to look at the portrait. Even Harvey would be satisfied with such a painting, but as I saw him squinting at my tableau, I knew that he wasn't. He tapped his finger on the window lightly.

"There is no latch on the window. No seam runs down the wallpaper, and you forgot the hinges on the door." Harvey stated, almost smugly, "Perhaps, you should quit while you're ahead."

Dumbfounded, I looked at the painting and saw that he was right. No one, I believed, would notice such things. It was a painting, not a blueprint. Harvey, however, thought differently.

"I don't understand. Isn't the point of any painting to make it beautiful and appealing?" I asked. Harvey took the brush from me and added some finishing touches, one by one. Finally, he spoke.

"When you draw on this canvas that you've heard so much about, you'll find that details are crucial. You must create a place so lifelike, that no one would spot the difference between what was real and what was not," he instructed. "Seems tedious, but a door with missing hinges would raise a high alarm in the Hotel Larouche. The people don't want to know that they are living in a facade. They want it to be real. So, I do my best to make them think that it is."

"Every room at the Larouche ... you've painted it?" I marveled, and he nodded not nearly as elated about it as I was. "How?"

"When a tableau is finished, you tap the canvas twice and the painting becomes real," he said. "It takes a lot of trial and error for me to get it just right," he said, still looking at my painting. A small smile begged at the corner of his mouth. "With some practice, you could get there too."

Slightly taken aback by his praise, I looked at the painting. *It had all become so apparent!* Finally, I understood the immense detail that Harvey's job required.

His focused demeanor paired well with the job he had to do, as it was no elementary task. A place like the hotel was full of details so minuscule they seemed unimportant. It was evident, however, that all the fine points were actually vital to the survival of the illusion.

The patrons, so lost in the scenery that surrounded them, needed to be fed a false realism to keep them feeling safe and secure. Without the details, they would start to recall their old lives again.

It was my thought, however, that with the canvas came never ending opportunity. It was both temptation and power, and I wondered how Harvey Nicholas had not come to get lost in it. He had worked with its magic for years, yet, there he stood wearing a slightly worn jacket, still powerless to his master.

"Harvey ... did you ever use the canvas for yourself?" I pried. Setting the brush down, he responded.

"Never." he said, leaning up against one of the stone walls. It was strange, but I found no reason to doubt him.

With much admiration, I regarded the finished canvas. Harvey had added a light shining in from beneath the door, along with a glare on the mirror. It was so secondary to him, I noticed, regarding the shaded creases in the curtains.

"It starts with a singular desire," he spoke up. "Man wants a home and then, eventually, a woman that he can possess and manipulate into loving him. He doesn't realize that she needs to eat to be kept alive. Eventually, he draws her a dining hall complete with meals beyond her dreams. A kitchen is added, then a carriage must be provided. Why not include a dance hall and a garden to tend? Then, of course, the man is bored of his companion and requires new friends!" Harvey exclaimed, "Eventually, you've become reliant upon the canvas, and it becomes your whole world. *Man becomes lost in it.*"

He set his paintbrush down and wiped his hands with a rag hanging off one of the barrels in the cellar.

"Our friend Larouche would be nothing without it," he stated, and then he looked at me and smiled, "but of course you know that. That's why I'm here after all."

For a moment, I felt guilty using Harvey as collateral in our plan, but I had to remind myself that what we were all in this for the greater good. Harvey, I knew, was one of *them*. From the way that he spoke about Larouche, however, I sensed that he held some suppressed resentment.

"Can you create life with the canvas?" I asked. It had been a question that I had pondered over for some time.

"Yes," Harvey said, hesitantly, "but life from the canvas is *soulless*. Any person made from it is not of this world and functions only as an accessory to the world you've created."

"How do you mean?" I asked, and he walked over to the tableau again crossing his arms as he observed it. "When you create something new, men and women will flock to it, eventually. You need to create a complete world before that can happen. Bakers, drivers, servants… they all need to exist to create the perfect scene. I call them the *Painted Few*."

It seemed unfathomable to create such beings, and I wondered if the Painted Few were easy to identify. Had I encountered one before? In all this, another thought occurred to me. As we stared at the painting of Matilda, I noticed that he had refrained from fixing any aspect of her. Surely I had left details out that only he could spot.

"Is there nothing to be altered or added to the girl?" I asked, gesturing toward the image. Harvey glanced at it momentarily.

"She would certainly do well as one of the Painted Few," he commended.

"Why?" I asked, slightly disheartened.

"It's all in the details, Andrew, or lack thereof. When you paint background players, you can distinguish them by the lack of particulars that make us *human*. You may find you meet a man with beautifully straight front teeth and nothing else. He doesn't have molars because they weren't necessary, to begin with. Some of the Painted Few exist without eyelashes and fingernails, the very details we would regard as naturally human. These members of society, if I would even call them that, are the most *inhuman* creations you'll ever encounter. It's what sets apart the real from the painted. Everything about them seems perfectly right, but is ever so wrong."

I couldn't believe what I was hearing. The idea that I had been living amongst these creatures was terrifying! My mind buzzed as I thought about all the hotel patrons and the men and women who served as the waiters, tailors, and bellboys. It was possible that each one was not of this Earth, roaming with the living as though they were. How had I missed it? Harvey interrupted my frenzied thoughts.

"It's amazing, isn't it, how taken by our surroundings we can get? We are so enthralled by what's happening and where we are that the details often escape us. That's why it's best to catch as many as possible. For the Painted Few, however, I don't worry about the details as much. I like knowing who I'm dealing with." He said, with some amusement.

The immense amount of work it took to create life was too vast to even comprehend. I wasn't sure anyone who hadn't devoted years of practice to it, could accomplish such a thing.

A place like the Hotel Larouche was full of trimmings and trappings so inconsiderable that they seemed unimportant. Yet, without them, the entire world Larouche built would *fall apart*.

Chapter Ten
A Tumultuous Friendship

"Can he honestly say he doesn't miss what we had? He treats me coldly as if he doesn't care at all."

It was Tansy, sitting by the fire in the kitchen, warming her hands. She had been talking about Patch for the past few minutes while I sipped my supper quietly.

"What do you think?" She asked, with large eyes. Secretly, I knew Patch still cared for her, but I couldn't betray my friend's feelings. *We, men, had to band together*, I thought.

"He followed you around for so long, Tansy. Honestly, we all sort of pitied him for it. I can't say I blame him for being ... *tired*."

She sulked, and her eyes narrowed in on me as though my reply was not entirely what she expected. In response, I added more wood to the dim fire, trying to stay in both parties' good graces by remaining impartial.

"It was wrong back then, Andrew. He wasn't himself! I felt as though I was looking at a man moment's from Death's grasp."

"So, you feel differently now?" I asked, and Tansy turned away, her eyes locked on the growing flame with embarrassment.

"Oh, I don't know what I feel. I was getting along just fine until I saw him that night." Her voice dwindled off, and I smiled to myself. All was *not* lost.

"Please, do not reveal any of this to him, Andrew. I'd die of humiliation," she admitted.

"I'm very grateful to you for allowing me to stay here. Everyone looks well, as though you've all found your purpose in life. It's so lovely to be a part of it! Life at the Hotel Larouche can wear you down, you know," she said, softly drifting into her own reverie. Then, as though struck by lightning, she sat up and rushed over to where I was sitting.

"What happened to your Matilda Brew?"

Taken aback, I had nearly forgotten about the time I introduced Matilda to Tansy. She had been the only person to meet her officially.

Suddenly, I filled with shame. I hunched over and felt a well of guilt within me overflow. Slowly, I pushed the bowl aside and stood up. The regret I felt never left me. It was always there.

"I couldn't tell you," I said, grasping the wooden table as a means of stabling myself.

"Surely, it's nothing so terrible," Tansy consoled, as she moved closer to me. My face fell into my hands, as I allowed the immediate feelings of despair I concealed to wash over me.

"I left her at the hotel. She seemed as though she were leaving forever, but not a night passes when I don't think about it. It feels wrong." I said, through a trembling voice. Admittedly, I felt foolish to be so shaken in front of Tansy.

"She's not gone, is she?" Tansy asked with worry.

"Somehow, I don't think she is," I said, and Tansy put her hand on my face, as to comfort me.

Before she could speak, Patch entered the kitchen. Quickly, I pulled away from his former lover in fear that he would misunderstand her kind gesture. Things were already tense between us; I didn't need him to find more reason to be cross with me.

Unfortunately, I sensed that I hadn't pulled away quite fast enough. Patch brushed us off, retrieving a small bowl and filling it with the leftover stew that was heating over the fire.

"What were you doing meddling with Harvey, Andrew?" He asked sternly, and I sighed.

"You know what we're doing, Patch. I needn't explain it to you again," I snapped back. He looked at me, and then looked briefly at Tansy who had taken up her seat by the fire again.

"Don't believe his stories, Andrew. You always were *too* naive," he scoffed.

"You were listening then?" I asked, not entirely believing that Patch *wouldn't* stoop to spying. "It stops today. Harvey's not to be trusted," he said, shoveling spoonfuls of the potato and leek soup into his mouth, with near fury.

"We need to learn from him, Patch," I spoke up. Patch slammed his spoon onto the table.

"Andrew Godfrey, you are nothing but that same boy I first met in the Social Hour. *Weak and naive.* They will devour your innocence because you let them." He said all this while pointing his spoon directly at my chest. "If you truly believe he's telling you the truth, then I'm all astonishment. You're even more foolish than I took you for!"

"Maybe I *am* more trusting than you, but you close yourself off to the world," I said, my gaze drifting over to Tansy. "You don't trust anyone but yourself!"

"That's because *I* never disappoint." He said to both of us, and then he looked at me, squarely, as if he truly resented what he saw. It was a look only found amongst enemies.

"I don't know you at all, Andrew Godfrey. All I know is *this*. You will lead everyone to their death. We will all fail because of *you*."

He left, leaving Tansy and me silent and wondering how things had gotten so terribly out of hand.

Father Caius had made it clear that Patch felt out of place amongst us. He reminded me that Patch came from a place where he felt useful and in charge.

What was left for Patch? Removed from his domain, stripped of his weapons, and forced to adhere to the commands of someone he regarded as *inexperienced,* the entire ordeal must have been humiliating to him. It was not in his nature for him to comply. Though I hadn't expected him to, nor did I want to force him to belong if he felt that it wasn't right, I had hoped our friendship would be *enough*.

The look in his eyes told me that it *wasn't* and, as the hours ticked by, I felt the resentment grow between us.

That night, I awoke to find Patch not in his bed. The church was still dark, and made it somewhat difficult see what was directly in front of you.

Stumbling, I walked out of the room grasping onto anything that was in my reach. I wasn't sure why I had awoken, but I knew I had to find my friend ... *if I could still call him that.*

Cold sweat trickled over my brow, as I began to fear the dark unknown presence that lurked in the shadows. What was I doing up and about at this hour of the night?

Cautiously, I made my way down the stairs. Stumbling down a few steps, I realized that I could plunge to my death and that would be the end of me. That would be all that the world would know of Andrew Godfrey, the shy boy from Howell Village. Inwardly, I cursed the blackness that blinded me.

As soon as I reached the last step, I made my way to the candles near the back of the church. I decided to light one with half a match I found while moving my hand back and forth over the votives. Scraping the head of the match against one of the stone walls of the church, the candle was finally lit and I was on my way. This candle would guide me to the sacristy where I would find Patch and all would be well.

When I finally reached the room, I found nothing. No one was there, and no trace of Patch could be found. Instead, *something else* caught my eye.

Straining to see beyond the dull light of the candle, I found my sketchbook lying flat on the table. Beside it, rested my pencil. *I hadn't remembered bring it down here.*

My hands shook, as I realized that something was dreadfully wrong. This book seemed as though it were placed for me to find it, as though someone knew that I would eventually come looking for it.

Slowly, I cracked open the first page of the sketchbook and breathed a sigh of relief when I saw some of the sketches I had worked on over a month ago. Flipping the pages, all my sketches appeared normal before they started transforming into sketches that *weren't* mine.

Sketches depicting death and destruction filled the pages of the book! Horrible symbols and creatures flooded the pages! In my terror, I found that I couldn't close the book, nor could I stop myself from looking.

The candle was flickering, and the floor beneath my feet felt like ice. My eyelids were heavy with exhaustion, yet I was compelled to flip to the next page.

With a gust of wind, the book shut closed and I was compelled to look up. In the corner of the room, just near the door, was someone standing very still.

I was petrified, as I realized that it was Monsieur Larouche calmly staring at me from the dark crevice where he stood!

Partially concealed in the darkness, I was still able to recognize his face. It was a face no person could forget once they saw it, with its bold features and piercing eyes.

He was wearing church vestments, a long white gown over a longer black one, with a cross dangling from his neck. In his hands, he was clutching a small black book and smiling cruelly. *The altar boy had grown up.* My mind saw what Larouche had become and it left me unable to move!

Hoping it was nothing more than a nightmare, I shut my eyes and I reopened them only to find Larouche gone. *No one* stood at the door.

Quickly, I held up the candle and spun around the room. The sacristy was empty and in it, I was alone and beyond shaken.

What was happening to me?

What was happening to my friend?

What had happened to Matilda?

My mind had created grand illusions even I didn't think myself capable of conjuring. Like a frightened animal, I ran from the room and bounded up the stairs.

Before I returned to my bed, I walked over to the window for some fresh air. It had been a night intensified by things I shouldn't have imagined.

Peering down, I saw Patch standing in the garden. He was drinking a bottle of wine and conferring with the moon, as though he were seeking its council.

To my surprise, I noticed that Patch looked distressed. It wasn't like him to feel any sort of concern for anyone or anything, but he seemed just as afflicted by the night as I was. While I watched him, I remembered precisely why men like Patch sought out the Hotel

Larouche as a refuge. It was the best remedy for days like this.

I didn't sleep that night. I couldn't. Wickedness surrounded me, and I wasn't sure *what* to make of it.

Chapter Eleven
Patch's Turn

The first sound I awoke to was that of two voices quarreling down below. Quickly, I sat up and swung my legs down to the creaky floorboards. I threw a jacket over my nightshirt and quickly buttoned my trousers while I stepped into my boots.

It took a few minutes for my eyes to adjust to the sun. *What time was it?* I thought. The shouts from down below were growing louder, however, and I knew something was wrong.

Desperately, I took the stairs two by two only to find Patch in a heated argument with Father Caius. In his hands, he held a small satchel and his hat.

"Don't you all understand? We left paradise on earth for this *dreary* place. This is no place for me. I'm heading back!"

"All you can think about is yourself. What about the others? They *need* you." Father Caius pleaded, but Patch scoffed at the old man.

"Need me? To what? Idly stand by while Larouche and his men tear us apart?"

"Be reasonable, Patch."

"Reasonable? I have news for you, Priest. I'm not reasonable, and neither is Larouche. I keep telling you that. If you walk through those doors unarmed and not prepared to fight you're done."

The whole scene was baffling to me, but not unexpected. This is what Patch often did. He fled when times turned and fell back into old habits as if they had been his best embrace. Now, he was about to leave us.

"Patch, what is this?" I interrupted, and he briefly looked at me, clearly irked by my interference.

"Well if it isn't *Michelangelo*, himself, come to lead us all to victory," Patch taunted. I noted a bit of jealousy in his tone.

"Is that what this is really all about Patch? You'll go with us, but not if you have to follow *my* lead?"

"No, Andrew. This is about getting out of something that is doomed to fail before we've even begun."

"Don't do this, Patch. I have never known you to be a coward!" I yelled as I noticed the others had begun to surround us.

"Maybe I *am* a coward. I've been called worse," he smirked, as he swung the satchel over his back. "I'm no artist, nor savior. I am but a man losing a war within himself."

"Remember your old life, Patch! Remember how miserable your time at the hotel was! Remember how you left with me, ready to be rid of the place!" I pleaded with him. This time, he looked at me as his eyes narrowed in on mine.

"I remember the music and the best food imaginable!" He laughed. Then he turned to the rest of the room and continued his proclamation. "I remember living in ecstasy, and never desiring anything! We danced! We conversed about nothing, and I LOVED it. I was foolish to leave it!" He shouted, and then turned and made his way out of the church.

"Patch! Stay, please! Do not go back! You will *die* there." Tansy said, running to him.

Coldly, he pushed her away, and she took a step back colliding into one of the pillars.

"Better to be a dead man at the Hotel Larouche, than alive here."

With his last embittered words, he left us stunned and feeling unnerved about the next few days. Someone among us doubted the plan and it was enough to arise skepticism in all of us.

Tansy looked at me with tear filled eyes, before excusing herself from the group. Valentina, noticing this, followed Tansy out, leaving the men behind.

"He's been drinking the wine and port in the cellar," Birch spoke up. "I found an empty bottle down there last week."

Father Caius sighed and began walking toward his quarters.

"A word, Andrew," he said, over his shoulder.

Immediately, I followed him, parting ways with Birch and Gideon.

That's when I recalled that Father Caius had something of importance to show me. He had mentioned it the day before, but now nothing was certain. Patch's departure from our group left a gaping hole among us, and I wasn't sure how the priest felt.

Father Caius's room was the smallest out of all the rooms behind the church. Hardly elaborate, his place had a bed with a writing desk and a bureau.

"Are you prepared for this?" Father Caius asked plainly, once the door was closed behind us. "Because we can stop all this now if you're *not*. No one will think any less of you, Andrew."

It wasn't exactly what I had expected to hear, but I appreciated the old man's honesty. He was giving me a way out, *but would I take it?*

Before I could answer, I took a seat at his desk and fiddled with the pencil that was on it.

"There is nothing else for me, Priest," I admitted, and he crossed his arms expectantly.

"*Now*, I have something to live for. Some time ago, I had a purpose to live each day and then I lost it. The Canvas took that emptiness I felt away."

The priest sighed, "If only I had done something more for Mr. Rhodes. There's good in your friend still. He's not what he presents himself to be."

"He is chained to the hotel … as most people are. If only we could make them see that," I responded.

Father Caius, suddenly remembering something, bent down and peered underneath his bed.

"What are you doing?" I asked, watching the old man crawl underneath the bed frame. One after another, he took out cigar boxes covered in dust and placed them on his bed. After he removed six boxes from below, the priest stood up and marveled at them.

"What are these?" I asked.

The old man didn't look up but merely smiled at his dusty treasure with satisfaction.

"This is our coup de grâce, Andrew. *The mortal blow.*"

Father Caius proceeded to open the boxes, each filled with pictures, letters, and small trinkets. He picked up one photograph in particular and held it up to my face.

"Look familiar?" He asked, and I noticed the old photograph was of a man and his alligator. It was a man that I had come to know at the hotel named Casper Vale. Beside him stood another man whom, from his apparent likeness, I could only assume was his brother.

"How do you have all this?" I asked, and the priest shrugged.

"You get to be a priest long enough, and people tell you things. They give you pictures of their long lost loved ones to pray over. They build altars to honor them. Through my research, I've been able to discover which of them lives at the Hotel Larouche...and, most importantly, *why*."

Suddenly, I was beginning to understand what Father Caius had planned. He was going to use the patrons' previous lives as a way to *free them*.

"I am still missing many, but I plan to collect more today, with Birch as a guardian. He may be blind, but somehow he knows these woods better than I."

It was an excellent idea, one that I believed could work if we were able to draw the patrons away from the allure of the hotel.

"You've outdone yourself, old man," I heard myself whisper as I sifted through the various keepsakes.

So many different faces and past lives had been collected and stored away for such a moment. I was wondering if such things could actually sway a person, but then I saw a picture of Patch.

With a medical bag beside his feet and spectacles resting on the rim of his nose, I scarcely recognized him! He stood tall, as one hand held his lapel with pride.

The back of the card had a note scribbled on it. Studying it carefully, I was able to decipher the erratic handwriting.

For the girl who dances with fire.

From the man who brought you back to life - if only to save his own.

Characteristically, it was just like Patch to write something self-centered and overly dramatic. I rolled my eyes.

"Ah yes, I remember that one," Father Caius chimed in. "You see, Andrew, many of us are so lost in the present we fail to see the beauty of the past. Good or bad, it has shaped us into what we are. There's a kinship there."

If Father Caius's word's held any truth in them, then there was still hope for Patch.

Disconcerted, I thought about my friend drowning once again in the chaotic lifestyle. *Would I save him this time?*

No, I thought. The only person who could save Patch was *himself.*

CHAPTER TWELVE
BENEATH THE MASK

"Hold still, Andrew!"

Valentina held up a measuring ribbon and proceeded to measure my waist and chest, while Tansy wrote down the measurements on a slip of paper.

"We don't have much time, *especially* if you want us to leave tonight!"

"At midnight, and not a moment later," I instructed, and Valentina nodded in response.

"Have you always been this tall?" She sighed, "I'll never find anything that fits you."

She and Tansy shared a look before circling around me slowly. I crossed my arms, only to have Valentina pull them back down again.

"The masquerades at Larouche are *garish*. If you don't dress like the others, you'll stand out," Tansy remarked.

Her spirits had dimmed since Patch's departure, but she was careful not to show it.

"I just want to blend in," I replied, blushing when Valentina took the inseam of my pant legs. She stood up and wiped her forehead.

"Trust me, what I make for you will be just right," she winked, then she retrieved what appeared to be the makings of a mask.

Black and tattered, it was shaped only to cover my eyes and nose. While I studied it, I felt Valentina tie it securely around my face before she handed me a mirror.

Once I saw my reflection, I took a closer look. It was a peculiar mask, in that it was unembellished and typically shaped. It didn't look like the kind of mask that a person would wear to a masquerade but more like a covering that a criminal would use to conceal his face.

Strangely enough, I looked like a man of great intrigue a man who lived in mystery amongst vagrants and thieves - and I had to admit that I *quite* liked it.

Beside me, I noticed Tansy and Valentina turn and whisper to each other, their eyes widening as they took in my appearance.

"I don't know..." I trailed off, shaking my head.

"He's practically *fishing* for a compliment isn't he?" Tansy said, rolling her eyes and Valentina laughed as she removed the mask.

"Til tonight, Andrew. We have lots to do!" Valentina said, waving me off, and then she and Tansy rushed away with the measurements.

Before I could respond, they were gone. I set the mirror down with some embarrassment, hoping that my attire for the evening would be downplayed and respectable. I didn't think I could handle any gawking.

It was nearly eleven thirty in the morning when I looked at my pocket watch. Father Caius and Birch had already made their way on to the next village, and my father had eaten his breakfast upstairs with Anais and Gideon.

Gideon was very attentive to my sister. With no eyesight, I wondered how he could grow to care for her, as she was essentially mute. Somehow, however, a sincere bond between them formed over the past few days. *Affection did manifest itself in different ways*, I thought.

***

"Why do you paint, Andrew Godfrey?"

Down in the cellar, Harvey and I faced a new canvas resting on its easel. I had decided to make room for another lesson before we were to leave at midnight.

We had been seated together in near silence before he posed the question. After a moment, I responded

"Because nothing was ever in my control until I picked up a drawing pencil and used it for the first time. It felt good to have one thing to myself as it was something I could command. Where my hand went, the brush followed because it was wielded by me and me alone."

"You like to control things?" He asked, and I shrugged.

"In some way." I said as I continued painting. Harvey circled about me, as he often did, criticizing my work with a strange sense of delight.

"Do you feel sorry that you could not control your friend from leaving?" he pressed. I had informed him about Patch's departure earlier. An odd sort of confidant, Harvey had proven to be a good listener. With Patch gone and my father occupied, I found that he was the only person I could talk to.

Still, I tried to keep my guard up around him. *He stands by Larouche*, I reminded myself. *He's here because he has to be.*

Reluctantly, I nodded, still sore with Patch's earlier departure.

"Loyalty is but a *myth*," Harvey spoke blatantly.

"I don't believe you," I said, shaking my head.

"Believe what you will." He retorted, and I looked at him expectantly. He couldn't throw around such proclamations without *some* explanation.

"I'm not loyal to anyone, to anything, but my craft," he began. "It's all that I know. Right or wrong, *art* is my master. It's why I have never abused the canvas for myself. Nothing else means more to me. Money, romance, people ... I feel nothing in my heart for any of it. It is all so unreliable, but art will never be disloyal. A painting's true colors are there for all to see, and only in its interpretation can it be worshipped or despised," he said, staring at the painting. For once, I believed him.

The way that he spoke was so unattached that it was impossible *not* to. He was an artist - he lived and breathed for it.

"If I may suggest it, you should devote your life to *your* craft. It's no secret that you have a gift," Harvey said, sounding as sincere as I had ever heard him. It took me by surprise, and I tried not to be fooled by his compliment.

"I intend to," I revealed to him. "But *not* without the canvas."

Harvey stood up instantly, as though he wanted to say something to me. Instead, he raked his hand through his hair and paced around the room anxiously.

"And what will you do once you have the Canvas? Paint *another* hotel with good intentions?" Harvey mocked.

Harvey then picked up the glass of water I had brought for him and drank it down. He slammed the cup onto the table and looked at the floor. I could sense he was losing his patience with me.

"We hope to create a union of men and women who find it in themselves to inspire others through their craft, as you call it."

I said this, almost lost in a trance. It was the first time I had said it aloud with conviction - perhaps, the first time the idea had really meant something to me.

We had been living in the old church for weeks, and I had almost forgotten what it was all for.

"How will you decide who will belong to such a union?" He asked, clearly intrigued.

"The good recommendation of others, I suppose," I shrugged.

We hadn't gotten that far in our construction of the union. I had envisioned a group of men and women similar to the rest of us who lived at the church. I had hoped that these new additions would be men and women whom I could call my peers *and* friends. Harvey looked at me, cynically, before turning away.

"People with *your* talent," I said, and Harvey scoffed at the flattery. Withdrawn, he leaned against the stone wall.

"People like me don't belong anywhere," he spoke, his voice just above a whisper.

"Men can change," I pressed, but Harvey merely sank to the floor and closed his eyes.

"They don't change, Andrew. Sometimes, they evolve into something slightly better or worse than themselves but I don't believe they ever *really* change."

Chapter Thirteen
The Midnight Escape

It was nearing the time when we'd make our departure from the church. A gloomy thought came over me, as I wondered if it would be the last time that I would ever see it. Though I tried to push such distressing thoughts from my mind, I had to face the reality of our situation.

It was an operation that *could* fail. I knew that, so I had to ask myself if I was truly prepared to risk my life for it.

The others in the church all bustled around with a nervous excitement. The energy was almost intoxicating as I felt us all propel each other forward, united, as we prepared to undertake whatever the following night would bring.

Father Caius was right. We couldn't stay here any longer. We had to flee in the darkness and wait out the daunting hours until we could finally enter the hotel.

Where would I lead them? I wondered. Without Patch's presence among us, my bravery wavered. Only *I* would be held accountable for the lives that made it through the night, and those that didn't.

In my anxiety, I didn't know what to do with myself. With a gulp, I made my way to my sister's room. My father had already dressed for our departure. His presence gave me confidence, as his calm demeanor eased the looming tension I felt.

Seated on the edge of my sister's bed, he looked up at me as I entered the room with a smile.

"Do you remember your brother, Anais?" He asked her.

My sister, who had been propped up with some pillows, looked at me and looked back at my father, somewhat lost by his question.

Then she buried her head in his shoulder with embarrassment.

"Give her time. She needs to get used to your presence," my father said, coaxing his only daughter back into the pillows.

"How do you feel?" He asked me, and I shrugged.

"I feel out of place. Everyone is counting on me and, yet, I can't understand why. They should look to *you*, not me."

My father smiled and shook his head. Then he stood up and made his way over to his belongings that were bundled together on a large armchair. I took his place on the bed beside my sister, who pulled the blanket up to her nose in fear.

"They trust you, Andrew. They believe in you," he explained.

"But why?" I asked. I couldn't understand it.

Years of blending in and fading into the background had left me wondering why the others had chosen *me* as their chief and commander. The real leaders were the ones who made lofty speeches and stood tall and defiant in the face of their enemies. With their heads in the air, they lead armies to victory because they possessed confidence like no other.

Those who knew me back home would never call me confident or charismatic enough to lead a camel to water, yet there I was prepared to rise and defend us all against the lions of injustice. None of it made sense.

"Mother would never believe it," I said, looking at my father. "I don't think she ever felt that I'd amount to much of anything. It was *Anvil* she felt would succeed," I said, recalling the way my mother used to favor my older brother. My father stopped what he was doing as he thought about the wife and son he left behind in Howell.

"Don't resent your mother, Andrew. She's had her share of difficulties," he reasoned. "I intend to visit them someday soon."

With a smile, my father picked up a leather shoulder harness and walked over to me. I stood up, wide-eyed, as he slipped it around my shoulder.

"You need this more than I do. Use it as the very last resort, when all else fails. Remember, they'll all be looking for for the boy who left the Hotel Larouche," he said, as he fastened the harness around my shoulders. "And the others he inspired to leave."

He then placed a small pistol under my left arm, and looked at me for a moment. There was usually a mixture of sorrow and exhaustion found when I looked into his eyes but now, as I looked at him, I saw something more. They glistened for a moment just before he looked away from me.

Before I prepared to leave, I sat back down on the bed and looked at Anais, still covered under the blankets.

"What do you think?" I whispered to her. "Do you think I can do this?" I asked her.

She looked at me, curiously, as if she was looking at me for the first time. Courageously, she sat up and touched my face while examining it. It was as though she remembered it from somewhere before. Slowly, I was becoming familiar to her.

She laid back down in her bed, but her eyes still remained locked on mine. Before I could say another word, our moment of recollection was interrupted by Gideon. He stood at the door, and cleared his throat as a means of catching my attention. I hadn't noticed him until then.

"May I come in," he asked, and I responded.

"Yes, of course."

Upon my reply, he entered the room, running his hands over all the furniture to ensure that he was close to the bed and close to my sister.

"They're packing up now, Andrew. I guess we'll be leaving soon," he said, sounding somewhat downhearted.

"If it's not too much trouble, Gideon, I should like you to stay with Anais and watch over her. I'll be going to the hotel beside my son tonight," my father intervened. He looked at me and I smiled. With that, Gideon perked up a bit.

"Well, if young Godfrey doesn't think he'll need me..." Gideon drifted, and he knelt beside my sister, taking her hand in his.

"*Stay*," I reassured him. I knew that it was where he wanted to be, and felt that my sister would be safe under his care.

As soon as we were dressed and ready to head out, my father and I made our way down to the garden together. We found Tansy and Valentina loading the cart with supplies.

"We've packed almost everything. There are only a few more items to load." Valentina informed us as we joined them. I noted an oddly painted gauntlet peaking out from under a blanket in the back of the cart, and looked at the two of them with suspicion.

"What is this?" I asked Valentina who shared a look with Tansy. She then walked over to the blanket and pulled it over the gauntlet and left with my father to procure the rest of the items. Our caravan was looking fuller than I expected.

Walking around to the front of the cart, I calmly pet the horse that would be pulling us along the way.

"This is it, boy," I whispered, nervously.

Nightfall was upon us, and midnight was quickly approaching. As the others continued packing the cart, I decided that it was time to make my way down to the cellar. It was time for Harvey Nicholas to leave the prison we created for him.

Upon my appearance in the cellar, he didn't stir. He merely sat on the floor in the corner of the room, staring at the adjacent wall lifelessly.

"It's time," I informed him, taking out the handcuffs I had brought with me, Quickly, I locked them around his wrists.

Without any reluctance, he obeyed, still lost in his thoughts. I could tell that he had much on his mind.

"Do not go through with this, Godfrey. Nothing good can come from it," he said, and his eyes looked as though they were almost pleading with me. "Return me to my master and leave this place. I will not speak of your plot to Larouche. You have my word."

His offer, I had to admit, *was* enticing. We had come so far, however, and I knew giving up was not an option. It would be impossible to convince someone like Harvey otherwise. He stood for nothing but his desires, while we all fought for something *more*.

Without another word spoken between us, I pulled him from the cellar. We were just in time to hear a soft ringing sound in the distance. It was a familiar signal that made my stomach lurch.

They were here.

Not a moment to lose, I made my way through the kitchen, nearly colliding into Gideon on the way. Carrying my sister, he was making his way down to the cellar where he and our lookout, Thomas, would remain until the intruders were gone.

"Be well, Andrew Godfrey," Gideon said, bidding us farewell. Silently, I prayed they'd be safe from any harm as I saw them descend the stairs.

We made our way to the garden to find Valentina, Tansy and my father seated in the caravan. We didn't have a moment to lose, I thought, as I walked Harvey to the end of the cart. He climbed his way in and took a seat beside Valentina, close-lipped and indignant.

It was as though he hadn't expected things to go as far as they had. Now that we were on our way to face Larouche, he had a choice to make.

In the distance, the sound of hooves trotting along the dirt roads grew louder and louder. Quickly, I boarded the front of the caravan beside my father and grabbed the reigns.

"Give me strength," I whispered, as I whipped the reigns forcefully. The horses began to move, and we were off. I took one final look at the church that had been my home for the past few weeks with fondness.

Looking straight ahead, I tried not to waver or look back at the church. I wanted the others to see me parading my courage and prepared to die. The courage *within me*, however, was fighting to *live*.

Chapter Fourteen
A Murky River

We traveled some distance before my father, who had checked his pocket watch, called out the time.

"Nearly three in the morning," he informed us, and Valentina yawned.

"Yes, let's stop for a rest," she responded, groggily. I had to admit that my eyes had closed once or twice, and my hands had occasionally lost their grip on the reigns. Exhaustion overwhelmed us all, and I knew the best thing to do was to stop for a rest.

We made our way through a narrow path beneath tall arched trees that looked almost menacing at such an hour. From my seat up front, I could hear Tansy speak to the rest of the group.

"Don't you know where we are?" She asked, her voice just above a whisper. No one responded.

"It's *Hanging Hollow*," she said, mystified by our location.

"What's that?" Valentina asked, and my father interceded.

"It's folklore, nothing more," he said, brushing Tansy's observation aside.

"Hardly folklore!" She retorted. "More people have been hung from these trees than fruit. I've been here once before when I was a girl. I was lost and stumbled through this place one evening. Though I didn't see anything myself, the cries I heard were real. We *can't* stay here, Andrew."

Nervously, I turned and looked over my shoulder for a moment. The rest of the group all looked back, their faces lit by the glow of the lanterns. Quickly, I snapped my attention back to the horse ahead of me and pulled the reigns.

"The sun will rise soon. We can't risk it. Folklore or not, *this* is our stop," I said, as our cart came to a halt.

From the slow way that the group moved I could tell they were each alarmed by Tansy's tale. I had to admit that I was doubtful of the woods and the secrets they kept, but I did my best not to show it.

As I grabbed the lantern from my father, I stopped when I heard the sound of a stream of water nearby. Tansy noticed this and grabbed my shirt.

"The *River of Lost Souls*," she whispered. "You must not go near it. The spirits of those who have ended their lives flow into the river and remain there always."

Tansy's warning was enough to send the us all to or designated sleeping locations. We rested on the forest floor looking up into the dark sky, and I breathed a sigh of relief. We had made it this far, and all of us were safe and sound.

In no time at all, the others had drifted to sleep. Only my father and I stood awake, listing to the sound of an owl's hooting. We rested against the trees, trying to guard the others while they slept.

"Andrew, don't believe the stories you hear. It's nonsense." My father said, concealing a yawn. After a moment, I could see his eyelids begin their descent over his eyes.

He was asleep, and I was alone with only the glow of one of the lanterns as my protector.

One fact about Tansy's story was true. There were noises in the woods, as though spirits were moaning collectively under the swell of the moonlight.

Only one thing kept me from turning back. One thought had crossed my mind since Tansy's telling of her horrid tale.

If the story *was* true, the lost souls were stuck in the river in the same way that Matilda's soul was captured in the mirror. Many listeners would find such a story peculiar and implausible but *I* didn't.

A sudden gust of wind blew out the flame of the lantern, and I was left sitting wide eyed in the dark beside my sleeping companions.

"*Andrew.*"

A whisper floated in the air that surrounded me. Squinting in the darkness, I looked at the rest of my group to find them all sleeping.

Without thinking, I stood up. *The river was calling me.*

If it *did* house souls then perhaps Matilda's soul was there as well. It was possible, I thought, that she had drifted from her place in the mirror into the river with the other spirits.

If Matilda was in the river, then it was up to *me* to save her. She couldn't remain in a place like this, so putrid and overflowing with decay.

Everything in the atmosphere seemed to speak to me that night. Cries and moans aligned with the sounds of the rustling leaves and rolling streams - it was deafening. How was it possible that the others could not hear it?

Finally, I approached the river. Standing at its bank, I looked across from me with squinting my eyes.

In the distance behind a thick fog swung the body of a woman hanging from a tree. Stumbling backward, I collided with the a tree's trunk only to feel something above me brushing against my hair.

As I looked up, my eyes met with a pair of shoes, attached to another dangling body!

Quickly, I ran over to the river's bank again. Careful not to fall in, I steadied myself and caught my breath. What sort of nightmare had I fallen into?

Slowly, I looked down to find not one body floating in the river, but *dozens*. The river was a stream of blood and despair as, one by one, bodies floated past me. Each had their eyes open as they stared up into oblivion, devoid of any expression as they drifted by in their eternal prison.

"*Matilda*," I whispered, leaning into the river. "Are you here?"

My voice trembled as a discolored female hand rose out of the water and clawed at the dirt of the river bank. The fingernails on the hand were black and rotted through.

Fear gripped me. Before I could move, the hand grasped my ankle sending me tumbling to the floor.

As I lay on my back, I could feel myself being pulled toward the river. Slowly, I felt the cold water run up my legs, as I was dragged down below. In the hysteria,

I managed to look up into the sky and see its full moon. There were no stars that night.

Wanting to scream, I felt another hand tug at my arm until, at last, I was completely immersed into the cold water.

The mass of death that surrounded me was sickening! I was wading through a pool of blood and misery. Whispers floated around me, as one dead body drifted by after another.

"*Death to Godfrey*," they whispered. "*He'll be among us soon.*"

In my dread, I opened my eyes to see a woman floating on top of me. Her long hair brushed against my face, languidly. Trying to pull myself up to the surface, I could see a thick welt like scar run across her neck. The rope had done its deed.

Beside me floated an older gentleman's body with similar markings on his neck. His gaze, void of any emotion, was a true terror when combined with his blackened mouth.

Struggling to free myself, I felt something in the water pull me down further. If *this* was my untimely end, then I welcomed it. My heart, my mind, and my soul were theirs to keep. All I wanted was for the anguish I felt to end. I wanted the screams and the guttural lamentations in the woods to fade away.

One by one, hands clawed at my face as I drowned further into the river. *They want me to stay with them*, I thought.

In the depths of such horror, drowning beneath a pile of decomposing bodies, I didn't notice a set of hands pull me from the river!

Suddenly, flat on my back, I gasped for air realizing that I   had been released from the shallow graveyard. Standing over me, however, was Harvey Nicholas looking quite severe.

"Would you care to join them?" He asked, stone-faced. Shaking my head, I noticed that he was still shackled.

"You can see them?" I asked him, and he nodded.

"Only those who mix with death can," he whispered, and then he pulled me up to my feet and started dragging me away from the cursed stream.

Though I wanted to ask him more about The River of Lost Souls, it was nearly dawn and I knew Harvey wouldn't speak about it in front of the others.

During our walk back, I wrung out my clothing as my teeth chattered from the cold. I looked back to see another swinging body in the distance masked by a black haze.

Darkness was everywhere, I thought.

Still, I could never prepare for the darkness I would encounter the *following night.*

Chapter Fifteen
The Final Lesson

When I finally woke up the next morning, my father had informed me that it was nearly one o' clock in the afternoon.

Everyone else had been awake for hours yet, I had let sleep and an encounter with the river get the best of me. Mildly ashamed, it was yet another instance of my incompetence as their leader.

Wondering if my confrontation with the lost souls had been some terrible nightmare, I looked over at Harvey who had been tied to a tree. He stared at me while the rest of the others ate. It was enough to inform me that my night might not have been imagined after all.

Awkwardly, I walked over to Harvey and sat down beside him.

"They all thought I tried to drown you," he said, dryly. I chuckled in response.

"You *saved* me, which is *far* more shocking," I replied.

He crossed his legs and leaned back against the tree as if he hadn't heard me.

"With *you* gone, the plan is off. If the plan is off, I can't ever return home. It's that simple," he explained, then he turned to me, his face oddly passive and unfeeling. With such an expression, I was forced to believe him. Foolish, was I, to believe he possessed any sympathy for our cause.

"You're wrong. They'd carry on with or without me," I replied looking at the others, but Harvey merely shook his head.

"You're the divine messenger, the *Archangel* in all this. You're bringing them aspirations for a better world, or don't you understand that?" He responded snidely.

We sat together in silence, each contemplating the crusade ahead of us. In some way, whether or not I wanted to accept it, I had been the beacon of hope for Father Caius. His acceptance of me was enough for them.

It was enough for all of them, except Patch. Deep down, I wondered if my friend had made it to the hotel yet and if he had regretted his decision. His disapproval of my leadership was evident, and I only hoped I would be able to prove him wrong. Maybe then, I could free him from the hotel. Maybe blind faith and talking about an ideal was not enough for him. Patch was a man of action. He had to see my true abilities to believe in them.

"I should like one final lesson," I commanded, cutting through the silence, "After tonight, we'll have the canvas in our possession, and I'll need to know everything I can about it."

Harvey cocked his eyebrow with surprise. "Oddly confident aren't you?" He asked, and I shrugged.

"Feigning confidence is the only thing I have going for me right now," I replied honestly, and then he twisted beneath the ropes around him.

"Tied to a tree, remember?" He responded, sarcastically, as if he didn't expect me to free him from his ties.

In one swift action, I walked over to my father's jacket folded neatly over the side of the cart. From one of the pockets, I retrieved a bayonet and proceeded to cut the ties around the tree.

"Andrew!" My father said, standing up.

"We'll be right back," I announced to the stunned group.

Quickly, I pulled Harvey to another part of the forest, far from the threats of the fatal river. We eventually settled upon a patch of woods where the trees created a leafy awning. This allowed the sunlight to pour in through small gaps in the branches.

Without a canvas or paint, there wasn't much to learn, I noted. There were still questions I had that I needed answers to, however. If I was to protect the canvas, I needed to know the many secrets it held.

How could I build a *creed* upon it without knowing its functions and capabilities? I wanted to master it and be capable of teaching others how to use it.

"I think you are struggling to find some sort of *key* to the canvas. There is nothing I'm hiding from you, Andrew," Harvey smiled. His expression seemed insincere.

"Is there anything you *can't* paint on the canvas?" I asked him, as he stood beneath the trees masked by their shadows. After a moment, he spoke.

"*Love.* You can not create love with it. You can only manufacture a way to find it," he said, and I wondered how he had come to realize that fact.

"*Anything else?*" I asked, and Harvey sighed with defeat.

"No, I don't think so," Harvey replied, though I sensed there was more he was unwilling to share.

There was something else I had meant to ask him. For some time, I had pondered whether or not I should bring it to Harvey's attention. *What would he think of me?* I thought. My desire to know the answer outweighed my embarrassment, however, and I decided to ask anyway.

"I lost someone close to me, and I was wondering if..."

Harvey shook his head immediately as if I had said something wrong. We looked at each other before he crossed his arms with a sigh.

"I'm surprised at you, Andrew Godfrey," he said, clucking his tongue, "You haven't even gotten the canvas yet, and here you are … using it for yourself. What would your friends think? What would the old priest think?"

Harvey raised his brow arrogantly as though he had just bested me at a game of chess.

"It was just a question, a thought… " I said trailing off. Deep down, I felt that he was judging my character and was glad to have found a weakness in me.

"You are no better than Meir Larouche, himself!" Harvey nearly spat.

Looking down at my feet, I felt that he might be right. It was difficult not to be tempted by the canvas and all its power. My chest heaved as I shrunk away with embarrassment.

Don't let him decided that you are something you are not, I told myself. Larouche and I were *not* one in the same. Harvey was stirring a doubt within me, and it was up to me to prove him wrong.

"Have you never lost someone, then? Someone you cared about?" I asked Harvey, who looked back at me with confusion.

"When you lose someone, you're always looking for ways to bring them back," I admitted, "I'm not perfect. I never claimed to be, and maybe it's a selfish act but I'm not separating men and women from their families and filling them with alcohol and delusion. Those are the selfish acts of your master. He fills the empty void inside him with the ruin of others. He feels accomplished and empowered by the disgrace of those who follow him."

Speechless, Harvey had nothing to say. He stared at me with derision, trying to determine his next move.

"Can you honestly say that you've never used the canvas for yourself, even if it was for a drink of water or an extra blanket in the winter?"

"Our lesson is over." Harvey responded after a moment, and he left our part of the forest, making his way back to the campsite. I could see that he was determined to separate his personal life with that of his profession.

Apart from his occupation, I knew nothing about him. I didn't know where he came from or with whom he came. Everything about him was unknown to me, and it would always be that way. Cold and relentless as he was, Harvey Nicholas was otherworldly in his own way. I felt it best not to decipher his actual character. Harvey lived his life as he wanted, tied to a man who could only ever bring him misery, *but why*?

Making my way through the forest, I saw the others sitting around a dismal looking fire. Cold as it was, it was nearing two o clock, and the masquerade was hours away.

"Are you frightened?" Tansy asked, and I turned to her.

"Would it disappoint you if I said yes?" I asked, and she smiled.

"No, the opposite actually. If you were *not* frightened, I would think you were lying. At least, now, we know you are honest. A coward, but honest." She smirked.

With a groan, I let my head fall into my hands, and she nudged me. Together we shared a laugh, and I was glad that Tansy could find the humor in our complicated situation.

"It could be no one else but *you*, Andrew," Tansy said.

"That's not what Patch feels," I scoffed, and Tansy shrugged.

"You're wrong. He feels the same. If not, he'd be with us ready to watch you fail. With no one to love and no one to inspire, there's nothing for Patch to do. He feels useless."

Tansy's observation of Patch seemed logical yet, I couldn't wrap my head around it. Our friendship, I had hoped, meant more to him than that.

When six o' clock drew near, we made our way toward the edge of the forest in the caravan. The tensions among us were high as the cart came to a stop again.

Far off in the distance, we began to see the Hotel Larouche! It emanated from the merriment taking place from within. My heart leaped when I saw it, and I knew the others felt the same way. Nothing could remove the feeling you felt upon seeing the Hotel Larouche. Its beauty was hypnotic, and its structure was unparalleled.

There was nothing in this world quite like it.

"We will get as close as we can to the hotel before we make our way on foot. Father, you will drive the caravan to a safe location before following us inside," I briefed, and he nodded in response. "We need to make sure that we are in and out before being seen. I believe the canvas is in Larouche's suite, carefully protected. We will wait until he joins the party to make our way upstairs."

"What if he never leaves?" Valentina asked.

"We'll have to create a diversion," I responded. "Either way, we're not leaving until we have the canvas in our hands. Once we have it, we leave the hotel and never turn back. Are we clear?" I asked the group as a whole.

With the plan agreed upon, we all realized that it was getting darker and we had to move quickly.

Valentina began to retrieve the costumes she had created from the back of the cart, and everyone immediately dressed as the sun started to set.

My father's mask looked of ivory. Stoic and straightforward, it's tattered structure created a dramatic image when he held it up to his face. His gray suit and modest cravat complimented it. It only took me a moment to recognize his face as Apollo, the Greek god of sunlight. It suited him well.

Tansy emerged from the woods dressed like a queen. She wore a mask that connected to an iron-like crown. She looked both beautiful and dramatic as she adjusted the long flowing cape around her shoulders, her hair loose and cascading down her back.

Valentina had transformed into an Autumnal goddess, her face masked by an array of beautifully colored leaves. Aided by Tansy, she stood tall as her dress was fastened behind her.

Tansy then handed Harvey Nicholas a mask, to our surprise, and he looked at her strangely.

"For the man who has no say in what he does," she said, lightheartedly.

He looked down at his costume to discover it was a golden half mask that only covered Harvey's nose and mouth. The papier-mâché had been so expertly done that it appeared as though the mask truly was made of gold!

He placed it over his face while Tansy helped him tie it in place. She then handed him a long coat made from one of the tapestries found in the cellar, and he put it on.

Finally, Tansy approached me with a twinkle in her eye. In all the excitement, I hadn't noticed that I had yet to receive *my* costume.

She held out a mask, entirely black and made of what felt like iron. It had two small lions near the temples and a fleur-de-lys in the center. The mask was designed to cover my eyes and the ridge of my nose.

She made her way to the back of the caravan and lifted a blanket which had concealed my costume.

Underneath the quilt was a suit of armor, painted all white. I couldn't believe it!

"We found it in the cellar of the church, among some other odd relics. There's more history to that place than you could possibly imagine," Valentina said, and she handed me the attire that went beneath the armor.

Behind a tree, I quickly changed into the underclothes before Valentina and Tansy arrived with the rest of my costume.

From the gauntlets to the chest plate, I regarded my costume as one that a person would wear into battle. It seemed appropriate for such an occasion, though I *did* hate calling attention to myself. Tansy assured me that I would blend in with the extravagance at the hotel, and I hoped that she was right.

The final piece of the costume, a spaulder, was placed over my left shoulder. It perfectly concealed the pistol I carried.

After they costumed me, Valentina and Tansy stood back in awe. I was mildly embarrassed by all the attention. After a moment, Tansy smiled at me and then made her way back to the others. Valentina stayed behind.

"Anything less wouldn't have been enough, Andrew Godfrey. This armor suits the person that you are perfectly."

"I'm nobody," I responded, bashfully.

"You are someone to me," she said, adjusting my costume while she spoke. "*To all of us.*"

Shyly, I thanked her and then followed her out to where the others were waiting. Immediately, I felt everyone's eyes lock on me, but not with ridicule. The way they regarded me was with a strange admiration.

"A born leader," my father smiled, and I took a deep breath."You should all be proud of yourselves," he said, and then he turned back to me. "Especially you, Andrew."

He beamed with such pride that I couldn't help but feel a surge of confidence. Maybe I *was* meant to lead them, after all.

"Father Caius and Birch will meet us at the front of the hotel when the clock strikes ten," I informed the others. It was all becoming so real.

My voice wavered from my nervousness. None of the others said a word but instead looked at each other as though they now realized the weight of their situation.

My father took the reigns, and Tansy sat beside him. Taking their lead, we were soon seated in the back of the caravan ready to make our way to the hotel.

As the cart moved, I began to wonder what it would be like to finally stand in Larouche's suite. Would the canvas's location be visible to me? I didn't expect it to be, but was prepared to hunt for the canvas all night if I had to.

Harvey sat back, clearly unfazed by our small groups' incredibly large efforts to bombard the hotel and capture its king.

"Is there anything I will need to retrieve it?" I asked.

Harvey looked at me, his face looking even more austere from beneath the golden mask. He didn't move but, instead, stared at me coldly before reaching into the pocket of his pants.

From it, he pulled out a small brass key with a burgundy satin ribbon around it. He held it for just a moment, before dropping it my open hand.

"Thank you," I replied, only by then Harvey had already turned from me, watching the long road ahead of us become shorter and shorter as we approached the hotel.

We spent the long ride over in silence. None of us moved or spoke a word for fear that we would break the spell we were all under.

We were close enough so that we could hear the music from the party playing jovially for all the patrons to join together in dance and song. I remembered the parties well.

So lost in themselves, they wouldn't notice a small caravan make it's way up to the side of the hotel. My father slowed the cart down and looked at me from over his shoulder.

This was it. *This* was our time.

Jumping from the cart, we decided to enter the hotel two by two to create as little suspicion as possible.

Tansy and Valentina made their way up to the swinging doors of the hotel, greeting the other guests as though they belonged. In a matter of moments, they walked through the doors and disappeared from view.

Once they were inside, I turned to Harvey and retrieved a key of my own. He looked at me, oddly, as I unlocked his shackles.

"What will you do behind closed doors, Harvey Nicholas?" I whispered, as I stared at him challengingly. "Only when no one is watching can we discover who you *truly* are."

When I removed the shackles, he pulled away from me and jumped off the cart. Together, we made our way toward the hotel.

Upon our arrival, we were greeted by a sea of masked citizens that were each dressed more spectacularly than the next. Finally, we made our way through the revolving doors.

Before I could leave the streets of Larouche, I took one final look at the night sky, hoping that it would not be my last.

Chapter Sixteen
The Masked Intrusion

Nothing had changed.

Being inside the hotel was like being in a familiar dream you've had again and again. It was a dream that ended cruelly but disguised itself with familiarity and blurred scenery. It was a dream that gave you comfort and, yet, made you feel entirely alone. It was the sort of dream that left you breathless when you awoke.

We were met at the door by Valentina who walked casually alongside us. Tansy stood some feet away, taking in the people gathered in the lobby. I wondered if she missed any of it.

As we walked through the crowded room, concealed by the masks we wore, we marveled in the Hotel Larouche's most exquisite pleasures. The smells, the sights, the extravagances, all of it had the capability of sweeping us in again.

Strangely masked men and women paraded back and forth between us. Tansy was right. A masquerade at the Hotel Larouche *was* garish!

The gowns were large and tiered like cakes, and the suits were each pressed and decorated better than the next. Patrons disguised as Poseidon and Neptune, draped in a verdigris bronze, graciously strolled by in their radiant gowns encrusted with barnacles and shells.

A tall gaunt woman donned a mask comprised of ceramic Birds of Sorrow that looked as if they were soaring from her cheek and making their way down to her similarly colored dress.

Venetian masks intensified the colors of the hotel, which I thought would be an impossible thing to do! I was wrong, however, as I discovered the array of pigments were entrancing me further.

Fearing that we would get separated, I took a hold of my prisoner's arm, and he shot me a look. Harvey wouldn't escape that easily, at least not then. We needed to buy as much time as possible before Larouche discovered our plan.

A mask comprised of three faces passed us by, to which Valentina whispered in my ear, "The ancient goddess, Hekate."

I had never seen anything like it before! Golden masks shaped like crescent moons and sun gods dance by. Men wearing the masks of past kings and tyrants flirted with the women who were disguised as carnival jesters and dead queens.

Patrons strutted around in their adorned outfits, some representing medieval cosmology while others implored flora and fauna. Various constructed masks possessed both angelic and demonic themes, while others bore the lush style of the romantic Belle Époque grandeur.

And there was Pierrot! The face of the well known sad Italian clown masked a tall and angular man, clad in a fur-collared coat, loose pants, and an undershirt.

Swarmed by a crowd gathered about him, he appeared to be telling an elaborate tale from the animated way that he spoke. Finding the attention the man drew peculiar, I ducked behind a few guests with full masks and listened in.

The man stood atop one of the poker tables and preached to the crowd, who all clenched their bellies from the uproarious laughter they couldn't contain.

"It was *so mundane*. Five minutes in and I wanted to bash my brains out!"

The crowd laughed again as the man lifted his mask and placed a fat cigar in his mouth. A sinking feeling hit the pit of my stomach as I realized the man was Patch.

"How foolish I was for leaving this place?" He said, kicking the poker chips off the table.

There he was in his true nature, I thought.

All was not forgiven, however, I discovered. A woman, covered in crystals and dressed as the primordial night sky, stood up as she finished her champagne.

"You *betrayed* us!" The woman yelled, spitting at Patch. He merely wiped the spittle off of his arm and met the old woman's face with his own.

"I was *spying,* you see. Keeping my eye on that bastard Godfrey, and that other bastard with the *one eye!*" He said, pointing to his own eye mockingly.

Upon hearing the sound of my name, the crowd around him all hollered and threw their glasses at the wall.

"We'll *kill* Godfrey if he ever shows his face again!" A hefty man wearing a mask shaped like a goat bellowed.

"He'll probably let you, too! He's spineless. Won't even carry a gun!" Patch hollered. I almost couldn't believe it was him.

Before I could walk away from the ghastly scene, I noticed Patch look directly at me. Whether or not he recognized me, I wasn't sure. After a moment he looked away, taking another sip of his drink.

"Keep an eye out, ladies and gentleman. He's around here *somewhere*," Patch warned, and the patrons all eyed each other suspiciously.

My time to leave, I fell back into the overflowing crowd in the lobby.

What had I done to lose such a friend?

Returning to my cohorts, I noticed that the walk toward the ballroom felt endless, as though we were trampling through trenches on a stormy night. It seemed as though we would never get past the crowd.

So much laughter and chatter bubbled across the room as people danced atop card tables and slid down banisters.

We were back in a seemingly fantastic place, but couldn't forget where it would lead us. It was all *too easy* to get lost in its rapture.

At last, we arrived at the ballroom where everyone was dancing while the orchestra played on. Larouche, I observed, was nowhere to be found.

"Do you think he'll come down?" I whispered to Harvey, who stood a few feet in front of me.

Harvey spun around so that our faces were inches apart. Removing his mask, he whispered so that only I could hear him.

"I'm leaving you now. My time with you has come to an end." His cold and unfeeling eyes willed me to do his bidding, and I released my grasp on his arm.

"Do not do this," I whispered back to him. "You can be *free*!"

For a brief moment, I could see him hesitate but he pulled his arm away and took a few steps back.

"Let me go, or I will reveal who you are right here right now. You know better than I that they will tear you apart before Larouche even has a chance to find you," he said, looking around at the patrons nearby.

He was right. I was being targeted by everyone and didn't stand a chance against them. No amount of explanation or reason would prevent them from dismembering my body and feeding it to the dogs.

With such a threat, I knew I couldn't stop him. His loyalty was to no one, so what had I expected? He would choose the easiest path for himself because he didn't believe in anything else.

Harvey bled back into the scenery as if he was no different from what he had painted. *He belonged here*, I thought. Everyone had been right about him. Only I was foolish to believe otherwise.

Looking around the ballroom, I suddenly began to feel ashamed of what I saw. Lewd and reckless behavior seemed to be everywhere. How many good men had fallen prey to this bedlam and how many of them were capable of being saved?

The couples, extravagant as they were, were bawdy and far past all levels of inebriation as they danced together. Some of them were hardly capably of standing upright at all!

Contrary to the patrons, the musicians were lifeless. They played their instruments with little passion, and appeared unfeeling. *They'd done this before many times*, I gathered.

Remembering what Harvey had said about the Painted Few, I sauntered past them and regarded their features. If they were no more than background players, would I be capable of noticing? Nothing looked any different to me. They appeared to be musicians, same as any that you would see at a party.

Then, casually, I walked around the orchestra and noted something odd. One of the musicians, a man with an auburn head of hair had it cut short in the back. What disturbed me most, however, was the smoothness his hair possessed. It was void of any lines or edges as if it were a blotch on a canvas. It, in no way, matched the hair in front.

Immediately, I looked at the other musicians down the row and saw the same likeness to the first musician's head. All uniform, their heads looked unnatural and almost blurred. I couldn't understand it.

"Psst, Andrew!"

Jarred slightly, I looked up to find Valentina, swathed in sapphire fabric. She looked stunning in her mask.

"Do you miss it?" She asked.

Taking another glance around the room, I responded honestly. "I suppose a part of me will always long for it, but I have to remind myself of the troubles it brings."

With a knowing smile, she turned to a nearby grandfather clock. Lacing her fingers together nervously, she looked at me with worry.

"Do you think he'll *ever* come down from his tower?" She asked.

During my stay at the hotel, I had frequently seen Larouche descend from his throne and make an appearance at the large parties the citizens threw in his honor but tonight, I knew, was different.

Larouche had to expect that there were men out there wanting to dethrone him. His guard must have been up, as he had something more to protect. It wouldn't be like him to leave the canvas exposed. For all we knew, Larouche may have decided to stay in his suite the entire night, but we couldn't let that deter us.

"It doesn't matter. One way or another, we're going in."

With that, she nodded and made her way out of the ballroom. Just as I was about to follow her something, or rather someone, captured my interest.

A girl.

My breath caught, as I took in the girl's appearance. Clothed in a black gown that flowed about her, the dress was offset by a unique ivory mask that snaked itself along her face as vines often do. Although her mouth was concealed behind the mask, the rest of her visage drew me in. This girl looked so familiar ... so much like someone from my past.

Her thick raven curls and large eyes lead me to believe one thing. In all my life, I had never felt such feelings for any other person in this world. My heart raced, and I just knew that this girl was unmistakably *Matilda!*

With no mirror to prevent her from the real world, Matilda stood among us as though she were alive!

Quickly, I felt myself rush toward her, as the girl looked back at me, almost expectant.

Matilda! In the flesh! I thought, breathlessly. I couldn't get there fast enough!

In a matter of seconds, I was standing over her, and she was looking back up at me. We exchanged no words as we each stared at each other, wondering if the other was real.

"M-M-Matilda!" I stammered, trying to keep my voice at a whisper. "It's me, *Andrew*!"

The girl didn't speak. With her mouth concealed behind the mask, I was unable to determine if her expression was kind and wanting. Struck by her presence, I gazed into was her eyes hiding beneath the curvature of one of the ivory "branches" of the mask. She lifted her hands up, as though she wanted to dance and I nearly rushed at the opportunity.

Without a response, I took her hand in mine. My eyes never left her. Her movements, her penetrating gaze, and her delicate but strong nature… this girl *had* to be Matilda! I could scarcely believe it!

My hand curled around her waist as I drew her close to me. Was there music playing? If so, I couldn't hear it. The sound of my heartbeat was deafening. So lifelike, I had to wonder if my mind was playing tricks on me. If so, it was the most precious of mirages.

"Matilda, I should never have left you here. You've always hated this place, and its vulgarity. Knowing that, how could I have left you?"

"Humans are nocturnal creatures, Andrew. We exist in both light and darkness, as we desire. Never blame yourself."

Her voice was full of conviction, precisely as I remembered it.

"How is this possible?" I asked, still in awe. Nothing else mattered but this moment, and I never wanted it to end. Gifted a second chance, I didn't want ever to let go.

Just then, the girl stopped swaying and looked at me as though she wanted to tell me something. I leaned in close and waited, anxiously.

Our dance was interrupted, however, by a piercing shriek that came from the lobby! The music immediately ceased. All the patrons stopped their dancing and began moving toward the commotion with intrigue. Reluctantly, I let go of the girl's hands.

"Be safe, danger's afoot," I warned her, as she let go. Slowly, she faded into the crowd, and I began to lose sight of her.

The screaming intensified! Shouts and gasps occurred collectively in the next room, and I worried that something in our plan had gone disastrously wrong.

In a few strides, I entered the lobby to find a group gathered in the center of the room. Quickly, I moved between the patrons. Valentina and my father were both beside me, and we looked at each other with worry.

"No tongue? What sort of trick is this?"

A woman was peering into a man's mouth, only to discover he had missing teeth and no tongue in sight.

"How is this possible?" Another man said, gawking at the others around him.

"Your jacket has no buttons!" The same man noticed as he pointed to a stout spectator beside him. "And no stitching, whatsoever!"

"What madness is this!" A woman shrieked, and her beau stepped forward.

"*Witchcraft!*" He shouted out to the rest of the appalled patrons.

Someone had tipped off the patrons to the idea that they were not alone. A strange species of men and women had been designed for their pleasure. They had been apart of a grand lie, and suddenly *everything was apparent*.

Larouche's deception was unraveling as the patrons were beginning to question everyone they encountered. Who was a friend and, most importantly, *who was not*? Who was one of *them?* It was enough to cause a near riot in the lobby, as the Painted Few were slowly becoming exposed.

I smiled as I began to realize that the commotion stirred in the lobby was just what we needed. *That would be our way in.*

"Remove your shoes," I yelled to the man from my place in the crowd, and the others seconded the command with their chants.

The portly civilian, without a word of protest, removed his shoes to reveal two deformed stump like feet. Harvey was right. *It was all in the details.*

Gasps floated around the room as men and women shrunk back in fear. Suddenly, everyone was suspicious of the other.

As if on cue, I looked up to find Larouche standing at the balustrades of the staircase, peering down at the calamity that was occurring. My father, standing directly across from me in the crowd, followed my gaze immediately. We looked at each other knowingly.

"What's the meaning of this, Larouche?" One man shouted to his master.

"Who are they?" Another woman pressed, as she clutched her partner's arm.

Larouche slowly came down the stairs, settling the crowd down with his hands.

"This is clearly some mischief brought on by those who have betrayed us," Larouche explained away.

As much as I wanted to stay, I knew that I had walked through the doors of the hotel that night for one thing. This diversion allowed us to continue our hunt undetected.

Discretely, I tapped Valentina on the arm, and we made our way to the elevator.

My father followed us out of the lobby which was crowded with frightened patrons. Everyone was shaken just as Harvey said they would be.

The only way up to the suite was the miraculous golden elevator. We slipped in, unseen, and breathed out a sigh of relief. We were almost there.

"Those people … " my father began, looking just as puzzled as the rest of the patrons.

"Creatures created to sell the landscape," I smiled. Valentina and my father looked at each other as though I were losing my mind. It wouldn't be a surprise if I were.

The elevator doors opened, and we walked down to the last room at the end of the hallway, only to find the door slightly ajar.

Carefully, I pushed it open and entered the suite that I had often imagined in my mind. Its decor was masculine and dark. The ceiling was elaborately designed and draped with embroidered tapestries that enhanced the gilded decoration. Wooden beams and a stone fireplace complimented the design that I knew Harvey had created some time ago.

The room smelled of smoke, and I noticed a small white bible resting beneath a burnt out cigar. *Larouche possessed a bible*, I thought. How ironic.

My father and Valentina instantly began searching the room for any traces of the canvas, while I made my way over to a corner of the room that fascinated me.

In the room, there were three doors. I had to imagine that one of the secondary doors led to Larouche's bedchamber so, in my curiosity, I pushed the door open.

As I walked in, the temperature dropped almost instantly. Detecting a strong foul odor, I looked up to notice dried bundles of lavender hanging from the ceiling in an attempt to mask the smell.

In a hardly furnished room was a large bed draped with a canopy of black muslin that fell to the floor. There were no windows in this room, I noticed. Only the light of a single candle bled into the room, revealing a thick blanket of dust covering the furniture. A feeling of emptiness washed over me, as I regarded the place as abandoned and hardly ever occupied.

One by one, my steps took me closer to the bed in the center of the room. My curiosity had gotten the best of me and I wouldn't allow myself to leave without a better look. What did those worn black sheets conceal?

Inching closer, I found myself reaching for one of the coverings, ready to pull it aside, when my father called out to me.

"Andrew! Come look!"

Pulled from my trance, I released my hold on the sheet. *There were more important things at stake,* I reminded myself. The mystery behind the black cloth would have to wait, I decided, as I rejoined the others. When I reentered the salon, I found them peering underneath a large object on the wall.

"There's something behind this mirror!" Valentina whispered.

Suddenly, I stopped where I stood. The mirror Valentina peered under was so similar to one in my past. The mirror was strikingly identical to Matilda's mirror! Apart from it being shined and polished, the similarities were *uncanny*.

Why did Larouche have it, I thought gulping at the thought that he may have known my secret.

Beneath it, was a door with a lock. This was where Larouche was concealing the canvas. *It had to be.*

The key Harvey had given me was safely tucked away in my sleeve, so I dropped it into my hand while the others looked on.

"*It's in here,*" I whispered.

We looked at each other with nervous excitement as we realized that what we desired was finally in our reach. Our moment had come and yet, it somehow felt too easy.

Was I to believe that we would retrieve the canvas and escape into the night unseen? Somehow, I couldn't fathom it. *This was not the end*, I thought.

Immediately, I stopped and put the mirror back to its rightful place.

"What's wrong, Andrew?" My father asked with worry.

"*His hands*," I breathed, recalling Larouche's descent toward the lobby.

It was all in the details; I recalled Harvey saying. Larouche, as he consoled the patrons down below, lifted his hands to settle them down. His hands, however, weren't what they appeared. They were missing something, an important detail that gave them a human-like quality. It was something that didn't sit quite right with me when I saw it initially. Now, inches away from the canvas, I found I couldn't look past the missing feature. Larouche's hands were missing creases along the center of his palms.

"That *wasn't* Larouche. Not really," I trembled, suddenly realizing we were in terrible trouble. "*He's here.*"

We all turned around immediately to find Larouche, a revolver in his hand, staring at us from the darkest corner of the room, his eyes almost glowing.

We stood there, each of us holding our breath as we watched the hotel's governor emerge from the darkness slowly with a cruel smile on his face. He lowered his revolver, slowly.

"He reveals deep and secret things; He knows what is in the darkness, And light dwells with Him." he recited.

From the sound of his voice, two large men came out of the third door on the far east side of the room. They flanked Larouche, and I immediately realized that we had been set up. Harvey had led them right to us.

"This ancient book would consider you the victor and me, the champion of defeat," he said, procuring the Bible in his hand just before dropping it into the fireplace. "But that is not the world we live in, Andrew."

Larouche approached us slowly then he turned toward a large window in the room. As he passed us, I carefully studied his hands. This time, there were creases on his palms. We were dealing with the man himself.

After a moment, he looked out the window gazing down at the street below.

"Are you the *chosen one* who frees the people from the bars that imprison them?" He asked. "Should I tie you to a stake and burn you like some patron saint? Crucify you *upside down*?"

My father stepped forward, but I used my arm to prevent him. In some strange way, this was *my* battle to fight. *I* had started a new reckoning the moment I walked out of the Hotel Larouche.

"Where I come from, people show no mercy. The men who fancy themselves to be pious philanthropists hang like angels. Their ribs are separated with an ax, and their lungs are pulled out while their entrails are on display."

An image of myself flashed in my mind immediately. It was a vision that was all to clear as I realized the horror of Larouche's threat.

Hung high above the fireplace, Larouche had turned me into a sick symbolization as I dangled from the wall like a piece of art. With my face pressed against the stone, an abundance of blood from the wounds on my back spilled down my back and onto the floor of the fireplace. He would have my body serve as a lesson to the others:

Infringe upon Larouche's sovereignty, and he would turn you into a carcass of pulverized flesh.

"You left my hotel with such false piety," Larouche said, pulling me from the twisted vision. "Do not expect to be welcomed here."

"I have no intentions of staying. I've come to collect what belongs to man."

Larouche turned from the window. The light from his eyes had faded. He had known about my knowledge of the canvas, I was sure, but to hear the words from my mouth was a confirmation. It was evident that he didn't find satisfaction in other people knowing about his contrived success.

"You must be so *proud*, Alben." Larouche sneered.

"I am," my father responded, rising above Larouche's mockery. In such a moment, it was everything I needed to hear. I stood taller and braver than before.

"It doesn't belong to you," I shot back at him. "It belongs to a good man and you *s*tole it."

Larouche turned back to the windows, opening them and taking in the fresh air. His two henchman stood back, never taking their eyes off us.

Another image came to my head. It was an image of Larouche dangling from a rope tied to the window. He hung from it, dead, as his gaze fell to the streets. People would look up at him, framed by his beloved hotel, with despise as he swung back and forth.

"I feel sorry for you, Andrew Godfrey," Larouche said, with feigned sympathy. "Forgotten in your hometown, you come here to make a name for yourself. You use the lives of others for your vanity."

"I come here to do what is right," I said, my jaw tightening at his haughtiness.

In Larouche's mind, he had already won. Our infiltration had only made him stronger, he believed, because what we desired most was in his power. He continually asserted himself with civility, as though we were less than the ground beneath him. Larouche wasn't used to losing, and he wasn't about to forfeit his beloved hotel to an insignificant group of nobodies. He'd rather *die*, and drag the canvas down to hell with him.

"I will put an end to your pathetic mutiny, Andrew Godfrey. *One by one*."

The heaviness of my gun seemed unbearable, as though it were beckoning me to use it. I could pull the trigger and Larouche would be gone, but then I'd be no better than he was.

"You resort to death as though you two are old friends," I responded, trying to find the courage to speak to the man who had long occupied my nightmares.

"Kill one man, and you're a murderer. Kill them all, and you're a god," he nearly sang.

He turned to me for a moment and then shifted his focus toward the man standing beside me.

"For instance…" He began, and in one swift movement Larouche pulled out his revolver from his jacket pocket and pointed it at my father's chest. Before I could stop him, he fired *two* shots. As I moved to shield my father, I heard a second shot ring my ears.

Two bullets had been fired - one that struck my father and one that hit *me*.

With blurred vision, I felt my body hit the ground forcefully. The floorboards then vibrated from the weight of my father's fall beside me. Finally, we were both on the floor facing each other as we awaited death.

All I could see as the room grew darker was my father's face. A single stream of blood trickled down the side of his mouth, while a muffled scream blared through the air.

It wasn't supposed to end this way, I thought, and then I drifted into total darkness.

Chapter Seventeen
Discovery

The hollow chapel beckoned to me once more, as its doors opened slowly. I walked across the cracked stone floor knowing that I had found my way back into the same dream once again.

At the precise time as before, Father Caius left his position at the altar and made his way to the spot in the center of the church. It was the same movement every time. Nothing changed, and I knew I was heading toward a dark and unnerving end once again.

I approached Father Caius in the center of the church, dreading what was to come.

As we faced the confessionals, hot tears sprung to my eyes. I felt hopeless, for there was nothing I could do to escape the fate that awaited me.

As my knees fell to the kneeler, I rested my head against the wall, with defeat.

"What is Andrew Godfrey's greatest fear?" Father Caius asked, and I nearly crumbled.

I was dead, and unprepared for what was to come. At that moment, I no longer feared Larouche. I despised him but no longer feared him. I didn't fear losing Matilda nor did I question her faith in me, as I felt that she'd always be there in some way.

Suddenly, I started speaking. The words poured out of me, free and unfiltered.

"I fear my family and their expectations for me. I fear that I will disappoint my new friends, and fail to bring them all that they desire. There is so much that I fear but mostly ..." I stopped, and my breath caught with realization. What I really feared was so evident. I had to stare Death in the face to realize it.

All this time, whenever I looked in a mirror, I was looking at Matilda. When she left, I no longer had a reason to look in any mirror. Most of the time, I think I subconsciously avoided them together as they possessed a gripping truth. All that was left in the mirror was a boy from Howell Village. I couldn't look in a mirror because what frightened me most was disappointing myself. I was never good enough, never smart enough, never to be remembered. I was everything the people in Howell Village said I was.

Peculiar.

Dull.

Uninspired.

"Andrew Godfrey's greatest fear is himself," I whispered. "My greatest fear is waking up one day and realizing that, after years of not believing it, I was in fact enough."

The confessional was still until I looked up and faced a reflection of myself sitting on the other side of the iron gate.

It had been some time since I had seen myself and really looked at the man that I had become. The person I saw seated across from me left me rather surprised!

His hair, once wild and disheveled, was still untamed but oddly well suited for the person he was. The painter's apron he wore was spotted with paint, and his hands were smudged in charcoal but he wore it well. I liked this Andrew Godfrey, whose confidence glinted beneath his kind eyes.

In truth, I wanted to know this man and become his friend. He held a secret in his look.

He wasn't gussied up like the boy at the Hotel Larouche once was, and he wasn't meek and frail like the boy from Howell Village either.

He was me, as I should have always been. Confident.

Suddenly, my senses awoke as I started to feel the carpet beneath me. The smell of Death, though not too far away, wasn't on my skin. I could practically taste life as the cold wind from the window hit my face. I was alive!

Opening my eyes, I found my father's lifeless body still lying on the floor beside me. My heart sank as I realized that, while *I* was alive, my father was bereft of life. He didn't need to fight that night, but he chose to despite the risks. He wanted to fight alongside his son, even if it meant his death.

My urge to rid the world of Larouche grew even stronger as I stared at my father's lifeless face. In my anger, I thought about the pistol tucked beneath my arm, ready to end it all.

Suddenly, a beam of light poured into the room as a door opened. I saw the faint outline of a man's shoes walked past me as I sat up, suddenly realizing I'd been shot in the shoulder, only *inches* from my heart.

With my hands tied behind my back, I noticed blood had stained the right arm of the jacket I wore. Like a slow stream, it had made its way onto the carpet. The mask that Valentina had crafted had fallen off my face and was resting on the floor beside me. It almost stared back, as though it were challenging me to rise and defend my father.

Valentina stood by the fireplace with her hands tied behind her back. She looked like Joan of Arc, defiant, even in the threat of the flames that surrounded her. *No more lives would be lost that night*, I told myself. *Only his.*

"He is *resurrected!*" Larouche scoffed from his spot in his armchair. "I have to admit that I was that worried that you were had left us before I had the pleasure of tormenting you further.'

He smiled, then he stood up and looked toward the corner of the room where a man stood holding a mirror.

"You should know, Harvey is quite the *'Judas Iscariot'* in his little act of betrayal. It was thanks to him that I even discovered your friend to begin with!"

My eyes narrowed in on Harvey, who stood proudly beside his master with my most sacred possession. I was wrong ever to have faith in him.

Larouche walked over to the mirror in Harvey's hand and took it from him, holding it up to the ceiling as he marveled in it.

"Fascinating, isn't it, that she should be so lucky as to have found rebirth through such an object..." his voice trailed off as he stared into the mirror, lost in thought. "Though some might see it as a curse, to look at life through the glass and always want to be a part of it."

Before I could shout out in protest, Larouche set the mirror down on his armchair and picked up his revolver from the side table.

Walking over slowly, Larouche pointed the revolver at my face. He looked down at me while he dug his boot into my wounded shoulder.

The pain was so torturous that I cried out in despair! Tears streamed from my eyes as I curled myself up under the crushing weight of his boot. I had never encountered such a feeling in my life, and I wanted, so badly, for it to end.

Finally, he pulled his boot from my shoulder and I gasped for air. In my desperation, I looked at Harvey Nicholas who watched me with little sympathy.

"How could you?!" I yelled at him, and he looked away from me. Larouche merely laughed in response.

"Silly boy, to think people *change* that easily."

Harvey crossed the mirror and slowly made his way over to me. Standing beside Larouche, they watched me writhe in pain on the floor.

"We were never *friends*, you and I," Harvey stated coldly. "But, somehow, I think you always hoped for it."

What had I done? In my naiveté, I had trusted Harvey. I had led us all down this dark path where we would die, one by one, as Larouche picked us off as he pleased. Patch was right and, in my stupidity, my father had been killed because of it.

The key, the canvas, and the hope were nothing more than false truths leading to a belief that good would always prevail.

They stood me up and untied me. Wilting from the pain I felt, Harvey placed a pistol in my hands and aimed it toward the mirror.

"How many others will you lose before you realize that there is no way out for you," Larouche said, walking around me as my hand shook with fear.

They wanted to crush my spirit by having me shatter the mirror and Matilda in it. They wanted me to destroy it just as they had destroyed the lives of those living at the hotel.

With great sorrow, I felt defeated as I lifted my weapon to the mirror. Though it was tarnished and old, the mirror held such a beauty. I would never see Matilda again, I thought. After I pulled back the trigger, I would lose her forever.

My arm fell to my side. *I couldn't do it.*

"Do what you want with me, only let them live," I whispered, as my lips trembled.

Larouche looked at me with annoyance, as he grabbed the revolver from my hand.

"You don't get to *martyr* yourself for the cause."

He turned and immediately pointed the weapon at Matilda's mirror. No time was wasted before Larouche fired his weapon again and again.

The first shot soared through the air. Then Larouche unleashed a second shot … and then a third. One gunshot after another resounded in the suite, as Larouche shattered the mirror. I felt myself open my mouth to yell, but there was no sound.

Just as he had done to the others, Larouche had robbed me of all that I fought for in this life. My father was gone and now, so was Matilda. I couldn't breathe. I couldn't cry. I couldn't even yell out in anger.

All I could do was pull out my pistol from beneath my armor, ready to end it all. Drained and exhausted, I knew we all would die if I stood by and did nothing.

As Larouche lowered his weapon, he stared straight ahead at the damage he had done disregarding the threat of my weapon inches from his right temple. It was as though he were distracted, I noticed. He looked over at Harvey Nicholas with confusion.

I, too, looked at Harvey who crossed his arms smugly as he watched. As I lowered the pistol, I turned back to Larouche.

All of a sudden, a bright ray of light pierced him through his abdomen, and then another! Larouche fell to his knees as he looked up toward the second mirror hanging on the wall with disbelief.

Two mirrors, I thought. One shone brightly underneath polished brass, while another remained tarnished and aged. From across the room, Harvey Nicolas stared at me. His cavalier expression had faded and melted into a knowing smiled.

Larouche had also been a prisoner of a mirror.

Chapter Eighteen
Long Forgotten

It was as though his soul were being ripped apart, piece by piece.

Another Triton of light carried itself through Larouche's side and then, eventually, *through his heart*.

Looking at him was impossible, as the light's intensity nearly blinded my eyes. No different from the sun, Larouche looked like a spinning wheel of fire! He was not of this world, nor was the unimaginable event taking place in Larouche's Suite.

Larouche looked around frantically, realizing he'd been tricked. Finally, his eyes landed on his most trusted companion, becoming conscious of the fact that this was *Harvey's* act of betrayal. The painter returned the look in silence, as his eyes reflected Larouche's ungodly decent into nothingness.

Black smoke waved over his body, pulling him from the earth. No man had ever witnessed such an eradication from this world and I wasn't sure what to make of it.

Before anyone could say another word, I rushed to my father and held his limp body in my arms. The weight I carried with me that night flowed into the body of the man I was to bury. My father's casket would close and so would any fears and doubts I had in me. He left this world believing in me, so it was only right that I do the same. *Enough was enough.*

From across the room, Harvey looked at me, and I stared back at him with gratitude. He had helped our cause for reasons unbeknownst to me. Silently, I thanked him, knowing that the artist could have *instead* chosen to remain in the comfort of his position at the hotel. We regarded each other, both exhausted and speechless, before he walked over to Valentina and untied the binds around her wrists. After he freed her from the restraints, Harvey turned toward the two guards in the room.

"You may go now," he commanded, and they left the room instantly.

Finding this peculiar, I looked at him, and he shrugged.

"The Painted Few have no *real* loyalty to anyone besides the person who created them," he explained.

Valentina, now untied, knelt beside my father and me. She shook her head as tears streamed down her face.

"Andrew, I'm so very sorry," she breathed, placing her hand on my shoulder.

"Your father was a good man, Andrew. Had I foreseen …" Harvey began to explain, but I quickly stopped him. I placed my father's body back onto on the ground and stood up, resting against the fireplace's mantle.

"You have much to explain, Harvey Nicholas," I said, trying my best to stand up.

He walked over to the polished mirror hanging in the corner of the room. He then pulled it down from its hook and scrutinized it.

"I always thought about fleeing this place, but I could never bring myself to leave. Larouche paid me well, and I used the money bring companionship to my life." With this, he looked to the floor. "It sounds odd, I know, but sometimes I would pay for a harlot just to converse with someone. Nothing more. The money gave me friends, and listening ears. It made me feel wanted and not alone. When you pay for a conversation, they really listen. They don't drown you out in their alcoholic stupor like the patrons do."

He walked around the room, running his hand across the mantle, before he spoke again.

"I told you that I have never used the canvas for myself, but that was a lie, Andrew. *I have*." Before I could speak, Harvey looked up at me, full of guilt.

"Funny thing about money," he said. "It requires so much fine detail that when it's painted it always looks counterfeit. I could never get it just right," he said, defeated.

"Larouche had me trapped and he knew it. Where would I go? What would I do? I couldn't convince myself that leaving would be a good thing," he said, recollecting his years at the hotel with bitterness.

"When I stumbled across the mirror in your old room, I took it as a sign. Its similar likeness to Larouche's mirror created a perfect deception. So, I tarnished *his* mirror and polished *yours*. The switch was done just this night, right before I painted a secondary Larouche to deceive you."

"Yes, I spotted the lack of details," I said, recalling the missing creases on his hands.

"I hoped that you would," Harvey admitted. "It was Larouche's idea to create another likeness upon my exposure of your plan, but I hoped you'd see right through it. Understand that I had to prove my loyalty to him so I could continue with my previous arrangement."

"Why now?" I asked, trying to piece together Harvey's story best I could. "Why tonight?"

"I had to know, Andrew." He said, with sincerity. It was as though Harvey was talking to me for the first time.

"They whispered your name around here like some crazed mischief maker. I had to know if you fought for the good of the canvas or the good of *yourself*. I didn't want the canvas to fall into the hands of another tyrant."

Harvey had no loyalties, I recalled. He admitted this almost immediately. His only allegiance was to the canvas, and it was logical that he would desire it to be kept in the safest and most trustworthy place imaginable.

Still, I couldn't believe the truth about Larouche. What I had witnessed was unlike *anything* I had ever seen in my life.

He handed me Matilda's mirror, and I took it with pleasure. It was nice to have it with me again.

"I don't understand," I said, bringing my hands up to my head in confusion.

"Your friend is not the *only* soul to ever be trapped in a mirror. There are a few cases where these things happen."

Valentina looked at me wide-eyed. She must have had so many questions, all of which would be answered in time. At that moment, I couldn't understand how a man like Larouche could maintain his power from the grave.

"I was there when it happened," Harvey spoke, as in answer to my question. "The night he breathed his final breath was not long ago, Andrew. It's only been a few years."

Harvey looked into the fireplace for a moment, pulling his jacket close around his slender frame. After some time, he pulled his gaze away and looked at me directly, as if he had something on his mind. In an instant, he headed to the bedchamber that I was in earlier.

Quickly, Valentina and I follow him, suddenly feeling the immediate cold as we entered the room. Harvey stood there, looking at the bed as if it had been some time since he'd last seen it.

"*Tuberculosis*," he began. "The Hotel Larouche had been in business for awhile and, when it happened, Larouche couldn't let go. He pleaded with his doctors, pitifully hanging on to every minute that passed by as if it were his last. He didn't want to go for fear that his heaven on earth would be replaced by everlasting fire.

"One day, *he was gone*. Only some of the Painted Few and I knew about it. It was my idea to bring down the hotel and permanently erase Larouche's mark from the world, but then *I saw him*. He was in a mirror, speaking to me! I couldn't believe my eyes! Such magic, such darkness, I thought I should release him and restore everything to the way it was for fear that he would come for my soul. He manipulated me, Andrew, and I was a coward for allowing it.

"I had nowhere to turn, and Larouche had always given me what I needed to survive, so I released him and waited. I would wait until his ego rallied against him and he brought demise upon himself … and here we are."

Harvey pulled the black canopy aside to reveal a skeletal corpse resting on the bed. Waxed sheets ran along his body, as in a desperate act of once trying to preserve their master's decomposing form. Covered in cobwebs, his skull was decorated by a crown of jewels. His clothing, similar to what you might find in Baroque art, was nothing short of *elaborate*. Rings adorned his fingers and emeralds decorated a faded silk robe.

The makeshift catacomb and the attire he wore were similar, I imagined, to what you'd find in the mausoleums of czars and sultans from distant lands. I'd never seen anything like it before.

"There he rests, in all his fineries, taking none of it with him," Harvey scoffed. It was odd to hear him speak frankly about his former master.

In Larouche's hands, I noticed, was a peculiar object. A tube-like silver case, about seven inches wide and twenty inches long, rested above his chest. It looked similar to the document carriers I had seen back home, only more ornate.

"What is that?" I asked the painter, pointing to the case. Harvey followed my finger and smiled.

"*That* is what you seek, Andrew. Half of it anyway," he said, as he pried it from the corpse's hands.

Finding the chain-like strap, he slung it over his shoulder and secured it. To my knowledge, the case appeared to contain the roll of hemp that the priest had locked away. It was something to smile about, as I didn't think we'd ever find it.

"Of course, you know where the rest of it is," he said, looking at the door.

Nodding, I walked past him and made my way to the open door retrieving the key from my pocket. On my way out, I handed the mirror in my hands to Valentina knowing I'd need both my hands to secure the canvas.

The others followed me as, with trembling fingers, I unlocked the small door that had been hidden beneath Matilda's mirror.

The canvas that started it all was inside just waiting to be used again and again. With it, we would create prosperity and happy endings for those who truly needed it.

As soon as the door was unlocked, I pulled it open and reached inside to feel a thick material beneath my fingertips. Energy nearly pulsated from the canvas to my body as a flood of joy washed over me. *There it was!*

As I retrieved it, I looked at the object in awe. Simple as they come, it meant so much to those that risked their lives to defend it. I held it in my arms and then looked over at my father. *He believed in it so much that he gave his life for it*, I thought.

There were so many questions that I wanted answers to and so much that I yearned to know. There was no time for conversation, however, as Birch barged into the suite, breathless and frantic.

"What is it, Birch?" I called out so that he knew we were present.

"You must come! It's Father Caius - he needs your help!" He said through gasps of air.

"We will take these possessions to the caravan and secure them," Harvey said, looking at Valentina who still held the mirror in her hand. He then followed my gaze toward my father's lifeless body lying in a pool of blood.

"I will come back for him. *You have my word,*" Harvey promised.

With such a vow, I didn't hesitate. I left the suite with the others immediately. We each followed Birch out of the door and rode the elevator down to the lobby.

"They've all started turning," Birch informed us on the ride down.

"*Turning?*" I asked, and Birch nodded.

"They've turned against each other. People are frightened with what they've seen," he panted, and I remembered that the patrons down below had encountered the Painted Few.

"You did this?" I asked Harvey, who looked at me and shook his head in response. Someone had to have informed the citizens that there were strange beings living among them.

"No, but whoever did was very smart to do so," he pointed out, just as the bell of the elevator rang.

The doors opened to reveal Patch standing there, with an arrogant smirk on his face. Suddenly, it all began to make sense.

"What have you done now?" I smiled, and he grinned in return. I should have guessed that Patch wouldn't *really* betray us.

It was *Patch* who enlightened the patrons about the Painted Few and the greater mystery behind the Hotel Larouche. He had infiltrated the lobby with whispered observations to those around him, pointing out what others had failed to see. I wasn't sure if he had planned it or had a sudden change of heart but I was glad to have him back.

"Well, ladies, I think it's time to get these people out of here," he chimed, slapping me on the back as I passed him.

"It suits you," he remarked, when he saw the armor I wore.

As we all exited the elevator, Patch extended his hand toward Harvey Nicholas.

"I have greatly underestimated you," he said, and the two men shook hands with a newfound understanding of each other.

We all ran toward the front of the hotel and walked out the doors with not a moment to lose. Stepping out into the harshest of windchills, I felt my eyes go dry from the extreme cold.

Harvey and Valentina met up with Tansy who helped them carry our findings to the caravan. Before she left, Tansy threw Patch a look of sincere appreciation, and

I saw him watch her as she left with the others. I wondered what had surpassed between them.

Beneath the moonlight were dozens of enraged citizens all howling at the old priest, who stood atop a carriage. A few of the patrons shook the cart with much force, as the priest struggled to speak over the commotion that was occurring.

Just before the carriage was nearly tipped over, a gunshot sounded and the patrons instantly fell silent.

It took me only a moment to realize that *I* had fired the pistol, pointing it high into the air, as the smoke drifted into the night sky.

The citizens all gasped when the saw me standing there, pistol in the air, angrily cursing me and wishing me dead. As they began to crowd around me, I felt Patch pry them off one at a time.

"Let the man speak!" Patch yelled at them all.

"Mr. Godfrey would like a word!" One man sneered, and another woman spoke up.

"He's the one who got us into this mess! Larouche will have you hanged from the lamp post!"

Murmurs floated amongst the crowd, as I began to realize that I had better speak fast if I didn't want to be torn apart. With a deep inhale, I spoke loudly for all the patrons to hear.

"Larouche is *dead.*"

At first, there was silence among them. Their leader had fallen, but could they believe it?

Harvey, who had rejoined us looked at them and they looked back. *Certainly, he would know the truth,* they thought.

"It's true," he said, looking at me. Soon, shouts and profanities followed. People were crying and shouting in the street, drunkenly cursing us all. Undeterred, I continued.

"The Hotel Larouche is *done.* A good man, my father, has fallen here tonight to protect something more, something bigger than you and I."

Looking down at my companions, I saw Patch look up at me, stunned and sympathetic, as he realized what had happened. Filled with conviction, I spoke words that I felt my father would have spoken.

"*Belief in Mankind*," I spoke, earnestly. The words meant something that night.

"There is no hope for us, boy!" One man spat. "You've destroyed the one thing worth living for!"

The unforgiving patrons stared at us indignantly, ready to pull the nails off our fingertips one by one, as they reveled in the long-awaited torture.

Another man grabbed a shorter man beside him. The taller man pulled his prisoner's head back, placing his blade at the man's forehead.

"I'll do it! I will! I'll skin you all alive if I have to leave this place!" He shouted, through the nervous chattering of his teeth. His face was pale and his eyes were crazed as the man in his grasp panted in fear. The men and women around him all stood back. "I'll fight and die for this place, and worship Larouche til my dying breath!"

Then he lifted his hand in the air, prepared to scalp the man in his arms. We all caught our breath, just as Patch shot the blade out of his hand!

"No you won't," Patch said, rolling his eyes. "The next man who speaks gets a bullet in the *mouth*," he warned, holding his gun out in front of him.

The shouts dimmed as the patrons all looked up at us. We were the enemy who brought down their fearless leader, and they would defend him with their last breath.

Such looks, such devotion, was to be admired had it been directed at a more lofty cause. To defend such a man, however, was evidence that these patrons had forgotten their previous lives and replaced them with an abundance of lust and greed.

"Larouche gave you the city of Gomorrah to blind you of your previous lives. He wanted to overpower you, and so he did," Father Caius spoke to the crowd. "I've visited a few of your loved ones. I have gone some distance to find keepsakes - mementos that will serve as a reminder of who you once were."

He held up two large handbags, and the patrons all regarded him as though he had lost his mind.

"Masha Reindhart!" He called out. A woman with short blond hair stood in the crowd slowly raising her hand with apprehension. How long had it been since she had heard the sound of her own name?

"Masha," the priest continued. "You were a *nurse* once. A good one, I hear."

"The best," she responded softly, but with pride.

"You worked under Doctor Monroe-" he continued, but she prevented the priest from speaking further.

"He took advantage of me!" She nearly spat. I could see the permanent hurt upon Masha's face.

"I'm so very sorry to hear it. You deserved a sympathetic ear and were instead scorned and shunned by those around you. Your *mother* is sorry, too. She's sorry for ever doubting you and wishes you would come home."

The patrons all gawked at the woman as they realized that someone among them was wanted back home. The desolate woman, so overcome by the news, fell to her knees and wept.

Upon seeing the bags of his collected keepsakes, I joined Father Caius up on the carriage and reached into one of the filled sacks.

"Jacob Adler?" I called out, holding up the next photograph. It was a portrait of a young man standing beside an older, severe-looking gentleman.

Jacob moved through the crowd toward my spot on the carriage. He looked similar to the way I did after a few months at the Hotel Larouche. His hair and mustache were expertly combed and worn with a touch of defiance and conceited independence.

"I suppose the old man has a thing or two to say to me, then?" he smirked, and a few men around him chuckled arrogantly.

"Your father passed last year, but he left *this* for you," I said, as I retrieved a small note from the stack of letters. I held it out to the wide-eyed man, who suddenly wilted into a grief-struck boy at the news of his father's passing. He reached for the note as he stiffened his jaw trying to maintain his composure amongst his friends.

"Jacob," Father Caius whispered. "I believe you may discover that the downfall of your father's business was never your fault. He knew that, too."

Jacob, a boy who believed that he had been the source of ruin for his family, took the letter with shivering hands and headed back into the crowd, reading it along the way. After a moment he, too, fell to his knees and hung his head low, holding the letter to his chest. So much time had been *wasted* at the Hotel Larouche.

He had missed the last critical moments of his Father's fading life all because of it.

Upon seeing such strong reactions from their comrades, the remaining patrons turned to me with a newfangled eagerness as they outstretched their hands.

Each of the patrons desired loving sentiments from their family. They each wanted a piece of their history returned to them.

"What is my name, boy?" An older woman asked me, while Father Caius handed out the keepsakes to the others.

Her hands clasped together with anticipation as I rummaged around for something to give her. At last, I found a photograph with a woman who resembled her perfectly. The back of the picture had names written on it.

"You are Emmalyn Grace! Daughter of Jane and Elliot Grace," I announced while handing her the photograph, and she nodded with the recollection of her past life.

"And what is my name, young man?" A rotund looking man shouted.

"Harold Becker, father of a two year old named Oliver!"

Father Caius smiled, handing the man a photograph and a pair of Oliver's mittens. The man looked at the small keepsake with such a fondness before he grasped the fact that he was a father!

"I have a son! I have a son!" He beamed. Some of the patrons around him smiled at the news, the bitterness they felt slowly melting away.

Suddenly, I was swarmed by citizens who had forgotten their identities and had long ignored their pasts.

Only when they were confronted with it could they discover all that they had missed.

As our group handed out the photographs, letters, and mementos, I could see one patron after another slowly make their way out into the black night, leaving it all behind them. With hope restored to them, neither the cold night nor the dirt beneath them could keep them from returning home. They were headed back from where they had each come from, perhaps, to some place where they had a second chance and a new beginning. Each person clutched the memento they were given to their chest, fearing it would disappear, as they left the Hotel Larouche. *They would never return.*

From their departure, I noticed that the magic that surrounded the hotel was slowly dissipating, too. The spell was over. The end of the magnificent structure was upon us. Slowly, I walked inside the hotel, facing a lobby now barren and quite and noticed something peculiar.

The Painted Few were slowly fading away. It was just as Harvey had said. Once the tableau was no longer needed, the Painted Few would be gone forever.

Waiters, bookkeepers, bartenders and even the concierge, *Phillip Bravery*, began to vanish. Suddenly, the wallpaper faded, along with the chairs and the tables. The beautiful centerpieces and ornate chandeliers disappeared, too. All that was left was the structure, seemingly ordinary in comparison.

"I suppose there's nothing for me," a quiet voice spoke from behind. Startled, I turned around to find a young man, no more than sixteen years of age, looking thin and jaded. The Hotel Larouche had not been kind to the boy.

"My parents both passed away, so I wasn't really expecting anything," he continued. Suddenly embarrassed, he began to walk away.

"Wait ..." I began.

The hurt I saw in him was evident but carefully concealed through a rough exterior. I felt terrible for the boy. Not only had life and the Hotel Larouche failed him, but in some way so had I. What consolation prize could I offer him? What act of kindness could I show to a boy only known the world and its cruelties? Quickly, I devised a resolution.

"Do you *draw*, boy?" I asked, and the boy shrugged.

He lifted the right sleeve of his shirt to reveal a tattoo of a beautiful ship with flowing sails.

"I drew this. It's the *HMS Victory*," he said, quite proudly. I inspected it carefully. The tattoo was drawn well, and almost looked as though it were moving across his arm. His attention to the sails alone was enough for me to find a place for him.

"This is quite *remarkable* … " I drifted, looking at the boy's face. "What's your name?"

"Thing is, I can't remember. I was hoping you could tell me," he responded. I looked at him again and smiled.

"Let's call you, *Alben*."

The boy grinned and he shook my hand with gratitude and a smile. We were then both joined by Father Caius, who crossed his arms and examined the lifeless hotel.

"We are ready to make our departure now, Andrew."

The old man placed a hand on my shoulder and looked at me with his one eye. I knew he must have seen my Father's body in the caravan.

"If only he could have seen this," he said, looking around at the remnants of the hotel. "It was what he wanted for so long."

My father was proud of me, I knew. Though our time together on this earth was short, he would always be with me.

"We should bury this place," I spoke aloud, but Father Caius shook his head.

"Why should we tear it down? The building itself is miraculous. Tear it down and you have robbed the world of something quite majestic. I say *we use it*."

"This?" I guffawed. I couldn't believe it! Had it not been the *net* that entrapped so many evils? Father Caius merely smiled.

"It serves as the best reminder that *light* shall always prevail over the *darkness*," he spoke.

The hotel had, at one point, been a home to all of us. We had each taken great pains to remove ourselves from it, yet now it was proposed that we return to it. I couldn't understand it at first, but then I realized something important. My fear had been *misplaced*. The hotel was a building. Nothing more.

As I looked at the hotel, I saw what the old priest had seen in it. The building itself was a beautifully built structure that we could only use to further our cause.

There were private rooms perfect for private dormitories. There were poker rooms and banquet halls that could transform into classrooms and galleries. Why start from scratch rebuilding something already available to us?

Any remaining evils and wicked spirits had gone from the hotel the moment that Meir Larouche had fallen to his death. The hotel was magnificent and would serve as the best of homes for our small guild.

As the days went by, I would begin to see the possibility within its walls.

What once was a glamorous hotel that housed villains and miscreants was now a home for artists who wanted to change the world with a flick of their paintbrushes.

The hotel was transforming into a glorious monument of opportunity before my eyes. This moment in history would be forever marked as one where a society of men and women rose from the chaos and *awaked the cosmos within.*

CHAPTER NINETEEN
BURIED FEELINGS

We buried my father the following day. The few of us in attendance did not cry, nor did we wallow in the sadness of the ceremony. It was not how my father would have wanted it.

We merely felt the wind on our faces and enjoyed the sunlight with a new purpose. My father had gone to sleep for the last time, protecting us all from a greater evil. We could not destroy that evil without him.

His body rested in his coffin, carved from pure oak, beneath a willow out by the chapel's garden. It was covered in flowers gathered together by Valentina, who had arranged them well. The ceremony, I felt, was more a celebration of his life than a final requiem.

If there was one thing to take from him it was his selflessness. He lived wholly for his children. His every thought benefited someone else. I knew the angels would come for him *gladly*.

"Andrew, what can I do?" Patch asked.

Patch and I had resumed our friendship the night at the hotel. It was as though nothing had passed between us. When I asked him if he had left the chapel that day knowing he'd come back, he turned to me and smiled.

"We needed someone watching out for you on the inside."

Looking at him now as he stared at me with compassion, I noticed a new calmness within him.

"Just be my friend. I don't think I could lose another person I care about right now," I admitted. Patch nodded and gripped my shoulder.

"You've got it."

***

The day we left the chapel, we gathered our belongings and rode out together toward a new adventure. The Hotel Larouche, or whatever we would decide to call it, was waiting for us and I had to admit that I was excited!

The only few who stayed behind were Father Caius, Thomas, Gideon, and my sister. They'd join us as soon as she recovered.

I'll admit that I had my doubts about leaving her, but I knew she was in good hands with Gideon. He cared for her and, in their own way, I felt that they had a kinship. It was for that reason alone that I felt that she'd be safe. In my father's absence, he had come to be a blessing to us.

The rest of the group traveled together in the wagon, each of us carrying a small satchel with our belongings. The change, though daunting, was appreciated. We had all been stuck in an odd sort of limbo and were anxious for our lives to commence.

Harvey Nicholas was already at the hotel, having made preparations for our arrival. He stood in front of the brand new wooden doors he had painted with his arms crossed, as he waited for us to reach the old hotel.

"Took you all long enough," he smirked, as we pulled the wagons to a stop.

"We hardly recognized the place!" Tansy spoke up.

"Just wait until you get inside," Harvey replied. Grabbing a few bags of luggage, he followed us into our new home.

What a difference!

This place was not gold nor was it decorated like a palace, only designed to host royalty. It was much simpler but strikingly smart and well crafted. The beauty found in this building was a beauty that you would only notice upon further inspection. It held a certain comfortable warmth that instantly felt like home.

A master artisan, Harvey produced furnishings met with both eccentric and neoclassical nuances that gave the place its originality. The eclectic mix of furniture varied from room to room as a blend of deep colored velvets upholstered the sofas and chairs. Bold and vibrant colored wallpaper replaced the elegant floral coverings of the Hotel Larouche.

To Valentina's surprise, varied Greek and Roman sculptures lined the hallways and accented the rooms. Spectacular art pieces and bookshelves gave life to seemingly gothic architecture.

Though this place was much more subtle than the gaudy rooms of the hotel, nothing about it was suppressed or insignificant. This was a place that was painted with pleasure and passion.

That fact alone was made evident in the various classrooms scattered with potted plants, geographical diagrams, and bright windows. Each dormitory was different and possessed a certain amount of character and charm. I had not been there but five minutes and I was already glad to live in it. For once, it felt as though it truly could be my home.

"Your room is up here, Andrew," Harvey said, guiding me toward the familiar elevator. I was grateful he hadn't gotten rid of it.

The ride up felt slow as I nearly brimmed with anticipation. We didn't say a word to each other, but I could sense that Harvey was eager to show me to my new room in the way that he fiddled with his pockets.

We got off the contraption and made our way over to the same room that I had previously occupied during my stay at the hotel. *Room 553.* It felt like years since then. Harvey unlocked the door and handed me the key.

"I hope you like it," he said, almost bashfully, then he pushed the door open.

The room was substantially larger than before. It looked similar to quarters that might have belonged to a professor, lined with books and a large desk. An antiquated globe sat on the end of it, while a deep green velveted armchair sat in another corner of the room.

Beside the desk stood my very own canvas. It almost radiated from the light of the window Harvey had painted. The view depicted a miraculous sunset glowing over lush green plains.

"There's absolutely no logical explanation for a window in here, but I couldn't resist," Harvey said, and I smiled.

A modestly sized bed sat on the other side of the room, right beside an object that was very familiar to me — *Matilda's mirror.*

Tentatively, I took a seat on my new bed and brushed my hand over the soft pillows.

"You don't like it?" Harvey asked, and I shook my head.

"Everything about it is absolutely me. You've outdone yourself, Harvey Nicholas."

There was a question that I had wanted to ask Harvey but I didn't know how. It had been gnawing at me for some time, but between the move and my father's funeral, I hadn't found the proper time to ask. Now, I decided, was the best time.

"That night, Harvey," I began, "I saw something - something that I didn't think could be possible. I still don't believe it but perhaps … "

"Andrew, may I speak to you?"

A voice intervened. We both looked toward the door to find Tansy standing there with her bag still in her hand.

After a moment, Harvey left us and Tansy took a seat beside me, looking around at my new room in awe.

"This fits you well," she smiled.

"It does," I agreed. I looked over to find Tansy fidgeting with her hands. *She had not come with good news*, I thought.

"I don't belong here, Andrew, that is I don't think I'm wanted here," she said, keeping her emotions guarded as usual.

"*Patch* ... " I sighed.

"It's fine, honestly, Andrew. I think I've known it along. I was clinging onto something that wasn't there," she shrugged. "I can't be where I'm not wanted, Andrew. I just can't."

Tansy looked down at her feet, and I put my hand on her shoulder. What could I say that would keep her here? She wasn't an artist by nature so she wouldn't be able to use the canvas. A place for her would be where her talents could be used and appreciated. A *dancer* at heart, she must have known that I had nothing to offer her.

"I don't suppose you'd be interested in *farming* would you?" I teased, and she shook her head and laughed.

"You are so good, Andrew. How did you ever end up that way?"

"Well, I really wanted to be a *scoundrel*, but it turns out that it's actually hard work!" I responded, jokingly.

Tansy laughed again, and then stood up.

"You are wonderful, Andrew Godfrey. Never change," she said, placing her hand on my left cheek.

Before leaving, she threw me a wink and left my room making her way down the elevator. I stood outside my door, just in time to see Patch moseying down the hallway.

"Where's *she* going?" he asked, taking a large bite out of a carrot. "Andrew," he continued, "that Harvey has outdone himself. My room is unbelievable!" Patch gushed.

It wasn't long before Patch noticed my deflated expression. He stopped and nudged me slightly.

"What's wrong?" He asked.

With a gulp, I felt terrible for what I was prepared to tell him. Though he would never admit it, the news would be devastating. As his friend, however, I knew that it had to be said.

"She's *gone*, Patch."

Patch looked at me, dropping his carrot onto the floor as his mouth fell open. He didn't speak but stood still in the hallway silently digesting the news of Tansy's departure and a life without her. Finally, he shook his head, clearly frustrated.

"The Hell she is! How can she leave without saying goodbye? How ungrateful can she be?"

He turned around sharply, stomping on the carrot as he headed over to the elevator. He bashed the button in with his fist and I knew it was best not to deter him.

Worried, I followed him down the elevator, listening to him rant and curse as he went.

"Unbelievable!" He bellowed, briskly marching out of the hotel.

Making his way onto the cobblestone street, he found her waiting for her carriage to arrive. She was alone with her bags in her hands, craning her neck to see if the transport was nearby.

"You're so *childish* - leaving this way!" Patch nearly spat, and Tansy immediately spun toward him with a flushed face partially concealed under the brim of her hat.

"*I'm* childish? You've been giving me the silent treatment since we met in the forest!"

Not wanting to intrude, I stood behind the church door. *It was best for them to confront each other*, I thought hoping they didn't *kill* each other instead.

"You don't want to talk to me, and then you *want* to talk to me! Make up your mind, Patrick!"

"Fancy that! You've been doing the same thing! You love me, and then you *don't* love me. It's enough to make a person go out of their mind!"

Just then, the carriage pulled up. Tansy readjusted the hat on her head as she prepared to board.

"Well, lucky for you, I'm leaving. You won't have to deal with me any longer!" She huffed, as she began to climb the carriage.

In three strides, Patch walked toward the carriage and pulled Tansy down.

"That's unfortunate because I'm leaving!" he said, beginning to board the carriage.

"No, you're not! Out of my way!" Tansy said, forcefully pushing Patch from the carriage.

"We can send for another carriage if you'd like!" The fearful driver reasoned after watching the two of them banter over who would take the carriage ride.

"That won't be necessary. SHE's staying!" Patch shouted back at the driver, as he pushed her aside once again. The action was enough to send Tansy tumbling down to the street, landing on her backside. She crossed her arms and kicked her legs out against the cobblestone in frustration, terribly vexed with Patch!

"Patch! You're the most *indecent* man I've ever met. I don't know why I even love you!"

Suddenly, Patch turned around to face her, no longer interested in boarding the carriage. Noting this, Tansy bit her hand as if she had revealed too much.

"You *love* me, then?" He asked.

"Yes," she said after a moment.

"Well, that's all you had to say!" Patch said, haughtily. I could see Tansy roll her eyes at him in contempt. "Get in the carriage," he commanded.

Tansy began to dust herself off, just as Patch extended his arm. She looked up at him, her face softening as she took hold of his hand. When she was on her feet, he moved in close.

"Where are you going?" He asked her, and she shook her head.

"I have no idea," she admitted, and he smiled.

"*Sounds fantastic.*"

Patch kissed Tansy frantically and with much fervor. It wasn't a long kiss, but I knew that it was only because they had much to catch up on and didn't want to waste any time.

The Hotel Larouche did that. It had a funny way of turning the days into hours and the hours into minutes. Now that the lovers could catch up, they were able to see each other for who they were *outside* of the mayhem.

They boarded the carriage together, smiling and looking genuinely happy. I didn't know when I'd see

Patch and Tansy again, but I knew they would be back one day.

For now, their whole lives were ahead of them.

Chapter Twenty
We Meet Again

One week had passed, and we had been overwhelmed by the tasks we had set in place to establish our new society. It was a week spent doing research and mailing out letters to artists who had caught our attention.

The contents of the letters we sent out were all similar and didn't reveal too much. We wanted the artist to be genuinely concerned about humanity's welfare before revealing the magic of the canvas. It was too dangerous to make any assumptions about a particular artist, and we felt that each should be treated equally.

Father Caius and I had crafted the letter together one night, each reasoning that less was more. The letter read:

To whom it may concern,
Should this letter reach the hands of a true and inspired artist - your expertise is desired.

If the preservation of humanity and the desire to do good on this earth call to you, then may we humbly ask that you join our society.

You will undergo a short provisional period. Your skill is a necessity, but your courage and strength are vital. These qualities are what we are looking for, and what we believe we have found in you.

In all this, you will find no monetary gain. You will find no publicity for your craft nor career establishing connections. You will do this, simply, for the pure joy that you find in it.

We look forward to meeting you.

Sincerely,

A. Godfrey

Nearly thirty letters had gone out and, after a few days, one response had been delivered. Quickly, I ran up to Harvey's room and knocked on the door.

With a pencil tucked behind his ear, he opened the door as though he were expecting me.

"The first one," I said, holding up the letter with excitement.

He didn't say a word but instead stood aside so that I could walk into the room.

His room was much different from the rest of ours, in that it was extremely plain and had almost no furnishings whatsoever. A simple cot rested beside his easel, and the floor was lined with newspaper and fabric. Harvey was a simple man who needed only the bare necessities to be content with life. I wondered, however, if he did not feel that he was undeserving of beautiful things. I sensed that he had felt some guilt in serving as Larouche's assistant for so many years. One evening I spoke honestly to him.   "You were not awake then, but now you are. We have all made our way through the Hotel Larouche at *some* point in our lives."

As he stood before me in his clothing spotted with paint, I could see that the man would live and die as the artist he always was. Nothing else meant enough to him.

"What are you doing?" I asked, noticing a canvas in the middle of his room. On it was a remarkable image of what looked like some contraption with brightly colored horses in it.

"Have you ever seen a *carousel*, Andrew?" Harvey asked, and I shook my head. I'd heard about them before, but none of us at Howell Village had actually seen one.

"It's all in the details, remember," he tutored, as I observed him.

Harvey must have painted the carousel for an hour, carefully selecting colors that flowed seamlessly together to create a vibrant and majestic structure. It almost moved, as I watched it take shape on the canvas. The horses were spectacular, as each beamed with a life of its own. At last, he picked up the canvas and walked briskly out of the room.

Down the elevator, he went, and through the front doors of the church. With a smile, I ran behind him. My heart leaped as I realized that I was about to experience something spectacular, something no person could ever describe!

We both hurried through the front doors, out of breath, and continued for a nearly a mile until we reached a vast piece of barren land.

Finally, Harvey placed the canvas on the ground and turned to me.

"With a structure such as this, you need open space. It's best to find a deserted area where your tableau will have room to breathe - *to live.*"

He instructed, and I nodded, unable to speak. I was too amazed by what I was finally able to witness. Everything had been so chaotic during our relocation that I hadn't had time to explore the canvas and use it myself.

Harvey retrieved his brush from his back pocket and bent down, tapping the canvas twice on its corner. I recalled him telling me that the taps were the only way to bring the painting to life.

Together, we stepped back a few paces and watched a whirlpool of color dazzle the afternoon sky. *Magic*, I breathed. It was the only word for it.

Watching such a creation unfold was nothing short of spectacular! I couldn't wait to test the incredible enchantment of the canvas for myself.

In a matter of moments, the painted horses fell into place on the great rotating machine, and I felt overwhelming emotion catch in my throat. This was something much more significant than any of us, and Harvey had known it all along.

"*Remarkable!*" I sighed. Harvey crossed his arms and nodded.

"Always wanted to do that," he admitted and, together, we watched the horses move up and down on the golden poles under the gleaming canopy.

"If we leave this rendering here it will *wear*, just as any structure would. Once it is among us, it grows old, like we do," Harvey reminded. "We must be careful with what we put out into the world."

"But what if nobody wants it? Will it then *fade away*?"

Harvey nodded and pulled out a small sketchbook from his pocket. He flipped through the pages, and I could see an array of illustrations used to create the Hotel Larouche.

Lamps, chairs, serving trays, and candelabras … everything created by the hand of Harvey Nicholas. It was amazing how much he had done and how lifelike it all was.

"There's something else, Andrew. Something I've wanted to tell you for some time," Harvey said, still staring at the carousel.

His face turned serious, and I wondered what was wrong. Had I done something I shouldn't have?

"You left someone at the hotel the day you fled. A girl," he whispered, and I nodded.

"Yes," I said, catching my breath.

"Andrew, we cannot bring back the dead. I've told you that once before," Harvey continued, and I nodded again.

"But there are *exceptions*. I was there the day Meir Larouche died, only to be resurrected again - *in a mirror*."

"Yes?" I pressed, trying to rush through all the fine details. The painter took a few steps back.

"The canvas is a *host*, same as a mirror. There is no difference between the two. This is how Larouche could coexist beside us, as though he were alive."

276

"Harvey, what does that mean?" I urged him, shaking him by the shoulders.

Before I could respond, the carousel made a full turn and something - or rather *someone* - caught my eye.

Standing beside one of the horses was *Matilda*.

A vision, she donned the black dress she wore when I saw her at the masquerade. It was the same dress she wore the day she passed. So lost in the miracle before me, I couldn't believe how something like this could be possible!

Quickly, I turned to Harvey who stared back at me in response. His secretive nature never failed to leave me surprised and full of wonder. With a small shrug, a smile played at the corner of his mouth.

"Go on, Andrew," he urged, and I smiled.

Like a man so lost in love, I ran with all my might to Matilda, who smiled and waved timidly. It seemed like I could not reach her fast enough.

"You're here!" I exclaimed, winded and disbelieving.

"I'm here," she responded.

"*Forever*?" I asked, and Matilda looked back at Harvey and waved. I saw him nod back, with a hint of shyness. Matilda turned back to me and beamed.

"*Forever*," she said, smiling. With courage, I pulled her close to me. It was magic to feel her again.

"I wanted, so much, to tell you," Matilda spoke into my shoulder.

"It *was* you that I saw the night of the masquerade. I thought you were a dream!"

"I get that a lot," she shrugged, and I laughed.

"What a journey this has been!" I said, covering my face with my hands.

"Well, you know what they say," she said, cocking an eyebrow, and I waited for her response. "If you can't handle the rollercoaster, *ride a carousel*."

She patted my shoulder, somewhat condescendingly, and I feigned being insulted.

"Are you saying I'm a coward?"

"Never! " She laughed, dancing around the horses.

I couldn't possibly explain why Matilda had come back to me. I didn't know how her soul had remained captured in a mirror or why I took her with me to the Hotel Larouche that one night. All I knew was that Matilda and I had *much* to make up for in life. Gifted another chance, she was with me and I would thank each and every cloud in the sky.

Harvey left us, no doubt heading back to his room to create again and again. So much had changed since we'd first met. I thought him so deceptive, yet, there was more goodness in the maven than I realized. Foolish, was I, to ever doubt him. Harvey Nicholas had given me the greatest gift of all.

It was miraculous to see her, to hold her, to kiss her, to laugh with her ...

She climbed onto one of the horses and beckoned for me to sit next to her.

We must have stayed out there until the sun descended and the stars took its place. Together, we spent the night dreaming up wonderful schemes and fanciful stories. We ran through the field, chasing each other until we were out of breath - just happy to be.

"I'll spend the rest of my life with you, Matilda, until the end of my time on earth," I promised her as we rested upon the grass.

"Death isn't the end, Andrew Godfrey. It's merely the beginning of a *greater adventure*," Matilda whispered.

That was the true magic of the canvas. Being with Matilda was an endless dream, and I knew she and I were going to be happy for a very long time.

One thing I realized that night was this:

If the canvas could create happiness for me, it could create happiness for others.

I couldn't *wait* to get started.

Epilogue

To whom it may concern,

I thank you for your letter. It was unexpected, and yet I had hoped for such a letter all my life. I believe that, through art, you can mold colors on a canvas into something as beautiful as the sun. What you offer sounds intriguing.

Are you certain that you have room for someone like me - someone who finds beauty in the common sunflower and familiar midnight sky? I don't paint ceilings. I don't sculpt gods. I live a modest life in Belgium, having sold a mere one painting. I'm not proud of who I am, or what I've done, but if you'll have me ... I should like to join you.

When you read this, know that I am making arrangements and preparing myself for a life with newfound ambition. To paint with purpose again sounds like a dream.

Sincerely,

V.Gogh

***

Some months later, we all sat around a large oak table with the inscription '*Ars Longa, Vita Brevis*' carved into the center of it. These words were from Hippocrates, and it meant '*art is long, life is short.*' I figured it represented us well. We were a new secret society and called ourselves *Canvas Carvers*.

Sitting around the round table like King Arthur and his knights, we faced our peers with excitement. We were all knights in our own way, fighting for a cause bigger than ourselves.

Finally freed from the hypnotism of the Hotel Larouche, the building still held a certain mystique to it. We were back in the old place with a new reason to live.

Harvey and I had taken the past few weeks to craft *fifty canvases* out of the roll of hemp that we had retrieved from Larouche's suite. The fifty canvases, plus the canvas used to erect the hotel, left us with fifty-one to distribute to those painters that were deemed fit to use them.

Father Caius sat directly across from me, his face glowing from the iron chandelier in the room that was slowly swaying back and forth. Valentina sat beside me, and on the other side sat Harvey Nicholas, focused and pensive.

The newcomers were also seated around the table, each unique in their dress, from lands further than the next. Sixteen men and women sat looking anxious and worried that we had lured them into some *devious* game.

As they stared at the plain canvases with doubt, Harvey and I exchanged a knowing glance.

They would never believe us if they were not shown proof, and rightly so. Everyone at the table had sacrificed to be there. Everyone had left something behind, and it was our duty to show them that it was not in vain.

They had each been tested and tried; their characters had been carefully examined. They had made it this far, so how could we not put a little faith into them?

Father Caius began after a moment. He took a long look at the people seated around the table, and the corner of his mouth began to lift into a smile.

"What we are about to offer you is a gift to mankind. It is not to be abused, but treasured and protected."

Gideon and Birch flanked the cabinet from the old church. It was the same cabinet that held a bit of the sky behind its doors. It had been transported to our new location a couple of days before the trials.

All our guests looked at it apprehensively, and many of them sat up in their seats with excitement.

Father Caius motioned for me to open the doors. Nervously, I stood up and cleared my throat. I still wasn't entirely used to leading a crowd, though *now* I knew I had it in me all along.

Still, the thought of everyone having their eyes on me all at once was somewhat daunting. I supposed it always would be.

As I walked over the cabinet, I spotted Matilda peeking in from behind the door to the banquet room, just as she said she would. I smiled to myself, suddenly feeling a surge of confidence.

Standing before the cabinet, I reached into my jacket pocket and retrieved the key. *Would I ever get used to this?* I thought. *Would I ever stop being amazed by the beauty within?* My hand slowly twisted the knob.

"What's behind this door will shape how you view the world, forever." I breathed. They all looked at each other with both fear and intrigue. "You can never go back to who you were before this moment."

As I looked at the group, I saw there faces, both eager and fascinated. There were old faces and young faces. There were faces of experience and faces of discovery. This magic wasn't mine. It belonged to *them*, and I wouldn't deprive them of it any longer.

And so, *I opened the doors.*

END

SNEAK PEAK

COMING SOON

***

It's never easy being the societal outcast in your twenties. It's why I moved to the city where I would be more readily accepted and blend in. Though it was never really in me to truly conform, I found that a *three-inch birthmark* on your face doesn't give you much of an option when it comes to standing out. I'm *always* standing out.

I'm a source of entertainment on the subway, something to watch in a restaurant, and a tinder swipe in the wrong direction.

If you think this is a story about someone's pitiful self-loathing you're wrong, but to set this up accurately, I need to start from truth.

An average looking person with a defect like mine faces some pretty deep shit. Life was never easy, and I didn't expect it to be. My face looked as if someone had taken a paintbrush, spattered it across my eye, and the paint remained there, permanently staining my face.

In the city, I worked as a cryptographer, or ethical hacker, testing major companies' websites to make sure they were secured from the actual conspiring hackers out there. It was a strange job, but I enjoyed it. It meant I could hide my face behind a computer.

I lived alone. I ate alone. I dreamt alone.

But I was Magdalena De Rossi, and I knew one day everything would figure itself out. I just wasn't sure how.

My parents lived in the vastly intriguing state of Delaware where nothing ever happened. Everyone in our neighborhood knew everyone else, and there was no hiding from them. There were no false identities that could be created or private lives to be had. *Everyone knew everything.*

It had been a few years since I had picked up my bags and left. As I grew older, I knew it was time to leave when I saw the neighbors look at me with pity. My parents knew it, too. They purchased my flight ticket for me.

So, I moved to New York where the streets smell like weed, and there's always someone passed out on the subway, because anything was better than *Delaware.*

Over the past few days, I began to feel something different. It felt like I *wasn't* alone, like someone was constantly watching me.

Anxiously, I would pull my trench coat around me tightly and walk with the crowd down the uneven streets. There was no reason someone should be watching me, just a gnawing feeling that I had.

Every time I'd turn around, though, I'd face a wave of New Yorkers walking briskly with there heads down, not willing to stop for anyone.

I felt this feeling for months, even when I closed my eyes at night. Someone was always there, and sometimes the thought alone was enough to keep me awake.

Early in the morning, I'd hit the button on the coffee maker and brush my teeth. Anxiously, I'd look at my reflection in the mirror to see if I could catch someone standing behind me. What was happening to me? Was I going crazy?

Sometimes on the weekends, I'd sit on my couch, drinking milk, and the paranoia would set in. Even through my glass, while I was chugging down the milk, I'd look to see if someone was there … watching.

Oddly enough, I was beginning to *love* going to work. It meant that I didn't have to be alone and left wondering if a hitman was after me.

It took me a while to get into the city, so I usually threw on the simplest outfit I could find and added some lipstick before I ran out the door.

Over the years, I'd begun combing my hair differently. I'd always tried to hide my birthmark by covering it with long bangs, but that got old. After a while, I gave the world a middle finger and started slicking my hair back. It felt nice to see the city without a blanket of hair covering my eye.

Usually, I could delve into a good book and ignore the spectators sitting across the bus. Today, though, I wanted to people watch. I looked around the people sitting on the bus in the early morning and wondered which of them were following me. From the way the train riders sat, earbuds in and eyes closed, I didn't suspect any of them.

Who could I turn to? Who would believe me? I had no friends, and my parents had enough to worry about with my grandfather and his dementia. There was no one I could confide in.

"Steve," I asked my co-worker one day. "Do people go looking for people like me? Would somebody want to snipe me?"

Steve spit out his coffee. Realizing I was serious, he looked back up at me and shrugged.

"I don't know. Have you pissed anyone off?" He asked, and I sighed.

I didn't talk to anyone, so how could I piss someone off, I thought.

"You should try Ritalin. My wife's on it. Works like a charm," he suggested.

Steve was a douchebag. I walked back to my desk and rested my head on it. *This is what crazy people felt like*, I thought.

A few nights later, I turned on the tv. Normally, I wasn't much of a tv watcher but, lately, it had been my best friend. Usually, I fell asleep with it blaring in the background. After a few nights, I began to leave all the lights on, and soon after … the blender. I wanted as much sound and light surrounding me as possible.

One night, I woke up to the opera scene in the Shawshank Redemption. I was sure that my neighbors were going to kill me as I looked up at the clock on my wall. It was midnight.

Sitting up, I felt the indents on my face created from the couch and yawned. Getting a full night's sleep was getting harder and harder these days.

Languidly, I stood up and stretched. I had to be up in five hours if I wanted to make it to work on time. Most nights, it was just easier staying awake especially after I brewed a canteen of coffee. Stupidly, I was running on less than ten hours of sleep for the week.

The window was still open, so I stood beside it, and enjoyed the fresh air in my apartment. The building controlled heating was creating a heavy sweat on my neck.

With my coffee in my hand, I looked out my window which faced a neon sign that read, "*It was all a dream.*"

Was this all a dream? I wondered. Was I so bored that I felt the need to conjure up ridiculous scenarios in my head?

Before I could think on it, something caught my eye. I dropped my canteen to the floor, as I caught my breath.

On the rooftop of the next building over, I spotted the figure of a man! His face was hidden by the shadows cast by the lights from the street. He was facing my apartment, standing incredibly still while he lurked.

After a moment, he dropped something on the floor and then left the rooftop.

My heart sank as I realized that I was *right*. Someone was watching me, and I was determined to find out why.